"I'm entering the fall festival baking contest. Are you?"

Mary jumped to her feet, whirled around to face Noah and lifted her chin. "Yes."

"Good. Game on, Mary. Let the best baker win."

"You make it sound like a kid's game."

Noah started to leave then stopped. "We both know there is much more here at stake than merely winning a contest. At this point, it's not even the money, is it, Mary? It's the title, the trophy and the prestige that goes along with the achievement."

"As usual, Noah, you've thought of it all." Her eyes challenged his.

"I'm surprised your bishop would actually allow you to enter a contest. It's such an open display of pride that you actually think your baking is that good that you can win a contest."

The surprise that covered her face told him she hadn't thought about that.

Yeah, this was not only going to be a game of skill, but one of wit.

Marie E. Bast grew up on a farm in northern Illinois. In the solitude of country life, she often read or made up stories. She earned a BA, an MBA and an MA in general theology and enjoyed a career with the federal government, but characters kept whispering her name. She retired and now pursues her passion of full-time writing. Marie loves walking, golfing with her husband of twenty-seven years and baking. Visit Marie at mariebastauthor.com and mariebast.blogspot.com.

Books by Marie E. Bast

Love Inspired

The Amish Baker
The Amish Marriage Bargain
The Amish Baker's Rival

Visit the Author Profile page at Harlequin.com.

The Amish Baker's Rival

Marie E. Bast

LOVE INSPIRED
INSPIRATIONAL ROMANCE

LOVE INSPIRED®

INSPIRATIONAL ROMANCE

Recycling programs for this product may not exist in your area.

ISBN-13: 978-1-335-43076-2

The Amish Baker's Rival

This edition published by arrangement with Harlequin Books S.A.

For questions and comments about the quality of this book, please contact us at CustomerService@Harlequin.com.

Love Inspired
22 Adelaide St. West, 40th Floor
Toronto, Ontario M5H 4E3, Canada
www.Harlequin.com

Printed in U.S.A.

With God all things are possible.
—*Matthew* 19:26

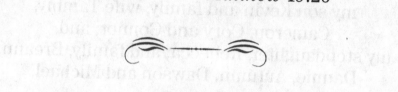

Dedication

My husband, Darrell; my son Brian and family,
wife Cynthia, Ezra, Ethan and Evan;
my son Kevin and family, wife Tammy,
Cameron, Cory and Connor; and
my stepdaughter, Rebecca, and family, Breann,
Dannie, Autumn, Dawson and Michael.

Acknowledgments

Special thanks to Melissa Endlich
and the Love Inspired team
and to Scribes202, my critique partners.

Chapter One

Washington County, Iowa

Was the rumor true?

Mary Brenneman hotfooted it to the front door, flipped the Amish Sweet Delights' bakery sign to Open and slid the dead bolt back. She peered out the window at the freshly painted storefront two doors up on the opposite side of the street, letting her gaze scour the words *Opening Soon* written in felt-tip marker on the brown paper still covering the windows.

If the rumor was true, and this was a fast-food franchise, it could hurt Sweet Delights' business. She raised her hand and blotted a tear at the corner of her eye. Just a year ago today, Seth Knepp broke their engagement so he could go live with the Englisch. Now it appeared she might lose the second love of her life. At twenty years old, she'd have nothing left.

Mary cranked her head to steal a better look.

The squeaking of cartwheels advancing into the bakery from the kitchen pulled Mary's attention from the window to her friend. "I wonder what's going in the new shop."

"Haven't heard," replied Amanda Stutzman, her friend and bakery assistant, as she pushed the cart toward the display case.

"Since bakeries started to pop up online and gas stations began selling fresh rolls and cappuccinos, Sweet Delight's business has tapered off. The bakery can't afford to lose more revenue." Mary huffed out the words. "We need to expand the menu."

Amanda started arranging the strawberry

and chocolate cupcakes on the second shelf of the case. "What's the holdup? Your *stiefmutter* and *vater* have been saving a long time for remodeling the bakery."

"*Daed* wants to wait until after they've paid off my twin sisters' premature delivery cost and their long hospital stay. Most of the bakery's profits are earmarked for medical bills."

Mary missed her *stiefmutter*, Sarah, working next to her. But after the twins were born, Mary had assured Sarah she could manage the bakery on her own.

Mary gathered her notepad and pencil from the counter, checked the sales schedule, and updated the blackboard with this week's Monday specials: donuts half price with purchase of a beverage.

She brushed her hands together to remove the chalk dust and glanced at the Kalona Fall Apple Festival flyer tacked to the bulletin board. Her focus landed on the events section.

Bakers! Enter the baking contest for a chance to win a trophy and the grand prize of $10,000. The main rule—at least one of your three entries must contain apples, and the apple taste must shine through.

Her gaze trailed down to the next paragraph detailing the contest schedule.

Each contestant must submit a baked good for judging by 2:00 p.m Thursday, September 24, in one of three categories:

1) breads, rolls, scones
2) pies, strudels, cakes
3) cookies, cupcakes, bars

Three winners from each category on Thursday will move on to make a different baked good on Friday. The judging panel will choose a winner from each group and those winners will receive $5,000. Those three will move on to compete on Saturday for the overall winner and the grand prize of $10,000.

Mary rubbed her fingertip across her entry confirmation letter clipped to her notebook. Ideas for a possible pie entry whirled through her head. But selecting the perfect, prize-winning apple dessert for one of the days wasn't easy.

After filling the cup dispenser, she glanced at Amanda. "If I won the baking contest, I'd remodel and buy the equipment needed to expand the menu. We'd serve breakfast croissants and biscuits in the morning, then switch to soups and sandwiches with home-made breads and buns for lunch. Maybe serve ice cream with pie. And we'd defi-nitely add an espresso machine."

"You'll win." Amanda headed back to the kitchen with her cart bumping the doorway and the empty metal trays rattling. "You're the best baker I know."

"*Danki.* This year the prize money will bring bakers in from Des Moines, Chicago,

St. Louis and all across the surrounding states. Many of them *gut* bakers from fancy pastry shops who have trained at culinary schools. I doubt a Plain girl with no formal training will stand a chance."

"You worry too much. Practice," Amanda called from the kitchen.

Mary sighed as she filled the cup dispenser. "I didn't win last year! Pastry chef Cynthia Návar carried home the prize."

The doorbell jingle jerked Mary around to the display counter. She laughed as Ethan Lapp pretended to stagger to the counter.

"Caffeine and sugar, quick!" He leaned into the counter as if he might faint without his morning breakfast. He removed his straw hat and put one hand under his suspenders as he slumped against the counter.

Mary laughed. "Your cinnamon roll is waiting." She handed him the bag and a cup of coffee.

Amanda appeared in the kitchen doorway and propped a shoulder against the door jam. "*Hallo*, Ethan." Mary caught the sparkle in her friend's eye and the special smile she reserved for Ethan. A frustrating sight, since Ethan never caught on to how Amanda felt about him.

"Hey, Amanda." He waved as he headed for the door.

Before the door closed, Frank Wallin strolled inside, letting a banging noise seep in from the street.

"*Gut Morgen*, Frank." Mary gestured toward the shop across the street. "Apparently, the carpenters are at it early today."

Frank removed his US Army veteran's hat and waved it in the air. "Morning, ladies," before pressing it back down over silvery-gray hair. "Mary, stopping here every morning is the best part of my day."

"Frank, it's *wunderbaar* customers like you that make me forget I had to get out of bed at 3:00 a.m."

Amanda pushed the pastry cart through the kitchen doorway. "*Gut Morgen*, Frank. It's always a great day when you stop by."

"Thank you, Amanda. Today, black coffee and an apple fritter, please."

"*Danki.*" Mary handed Frank his coffee and paper bag as he laid the correct amount on the counter.

"My pleasure. When is the new farm-fresh grocery and deli opening?"

Mary jerked her gaze from the money to face Frank. "What grocery and deli?"

"The new store across the street. They're raising the sign into place now. Sorry, but I need to get to work. See for yourself." Frank hurried to the door and motioned across the street.

She darted from behind the counter and caught the door as it closed. "It can't be! Where did that sign come from?" Tears pressed against the corners of her eyes.

"What sign?" Amanda pushed a new tray of pastries into the display case.

"The empty shop across the street, they've hung a sign. It has cloth covering the name, but it's ripped." She paused and squinted through the dust hanging in the air from the hammering into the bricks on the old building. "I can see the words *Farm-fresh Grocery* and *Deli*."

Amanda ran around the cart and peered out the window. "*Daed* is going to be disappointed. He was hoping for a hardware store."

"If they carry breakfast biscuits and sandwiches, and have a microwave to warm them, they'll steal some of our morning customers." Mary slumped against the door. The news sliced another piece from her heart, like Seth when he dumped her on the eve of their wedding. "By the time I get the money to expand, our customers will be across the street and gone."

"*Nein*, not true, Mary. Everyone knows you're a fantastic baker. Your customers will stick by you. Besides they can go to the deli one day, and your shop the next."

"Even that will cut my revenue. I have to win that baking contest next month, or Sweet Delights will die an embarrassing death. That gives me six weeks to practice."

Amanda wandered back to the cart and finished unloading the pastries. "Don't worry. The bakery has loyal customers."

When the door opened again, Amanda tossed Mary an encouraging smile then pushed her cart to the kitchen.

A stream of morning customers rushed in and out, many making excited remarks to Mary about the new grocery. When the bakery was empty again, she stepped to the door and stole another look across the street. Old Bishop Ropp sauntered up and entered as Mary held the door open.

"*Gut Morgen*, Mary. Looks like some big excitement in town."

"I'm afraid so."

The bishop stopped short and faced her. "Nonsense. Your baking is *wunderbaar*. Don't be afraid of a little competition. Now if you would serve me a slice of that apple pie that Sarah's *vater* used to make, my day would be perfect. I would drive my buggy five miles in the rain for a piece of that pie."

"Sorry, I have a country apple, but it's my

recipe. I'll have to ask *Mamm* about the one her *vater* made."

"Then I'll take an apple fritter and coffee." His smile stretched ear to ear.

Around midmorning, a young girl sailed toward the counter wearing jeans and a T-shirt and holding a five-dollar bill firmly in her fist.

"*Hallo*," Mary greeted her, "and what can I get you today?"

The little girl walked back and forth in front of the display case, smiling. "I don't know what to pick. It all looks good."

Mary nodded. "*Jah*, they are all *wunderbaar*. Take your time. I'm Mary, what's your name? I don't think I've seen you in here before."

"I'm Emily Miller. I'm eight years old. Most people ask since I'm small for my age." She pointed to the second shelf. "What kind of cupcake is the one with the pink frosting?"

"Strawberry, and I'll let you in on a secret. The inside has a strawberry surprise."

Emily's eyes scanned the pastries but a smile pulled at the corners of her mouth, then spread across her cheeks. "Okay, I'll have the pink one and a glass of milk."

"You can sit, and I'll bring it to the table." Mary pulled the treat from the case with her tongs and poured a cup of milk. She set them both in front of Emily and sat across from her. "Did you just move to town?"

"Uh-huh, my brother, Noah, moved my sister Jenny and me here from Iowa City. He's looking for a relative."

An *Englisch* person could just drive his car if he wanted to see a relative. He didn't have to move to do that. But Emily probably misunderstood what her brother said. "Did your *mamm* and *daed* move, too?"

"No, they died a year ago in a car accident." Emily's voice quaked. "It's just my brother, Noah, Jenny and me."

"I'm so sorry to hear that about your parents."

"You talk funny." Emily laughed, then took a bite of cupcake. "Mmm, this is delicious." She took another bite, followed by a sip of milk.

The bakery door opened and a six-foot-tall man eyed Emily and her cupcake and gave a nod to Mary. "That looks good. I'll have the same as my sister if you please?"

"Good choice." Mary scooted back to the display case, her heart nearly buckling as she watched the cute man stroll through her shop. She tore her gaze away. After Seth canceled their wedding a year ago, she wasn't ready for another relationship. Not yet. And certainly not with an *Englischer*.

The tall stranger glanced at the chalkboard with the daily specials and then glanced at the bulletin board and the fall festival flyer, where he skimmed his finger down the listing of events. He turned and scanned the display case as he sauntered over to the table, pulled out a chair and sat next to Emily.

Mary pulled another strawberry cupcake from the case and poured a glass of milk. "Emily and I were just getting acquainted.

I'm Mary Brenneman, and you must be Noah."

"Pleased to meet you, Mary."

His amber eyes caught her gaze and held it for a second before she jerked away. It sent a twinge straight to her heart. *Jah*, he was handsome, that was for sure and certain. His short, dark brown hair was the same color as his beard. It wasn't a long beard like that of Amish men but short and trimmed close, like what the *Englisch* called a five o'clock shadow. But it looked nice on him.

Emily held up what was left of her cupcake. "This was *wow-wee*, Noah," she mumbled, a couple of crumbs dropping from her chin.

Amanda hurried in from the kitchen and shoved a tray of sugar cookies into the display case. "Don't forget to introduce me," she said to Mary.

"*Jah*, Amanda Stutzman is my assistant and right hand. This is Noah and Emily Miller. They are new in town."

"Nice to meet you, Amanda," Noah said.

"And nice to meet you both." Amanda smiled and headed back to the kitchen.

Mary set Noah's order in front of him, trying to steady her hand. "Enjoy. They are on the *haus*, my way of saying *willkommen* to town. And tell Jenny to stop by for her cupcake. Emily said you moved here from Iowa City."

"Thanks, I will. It looks like I got here just in time, before Emily spilled the family secrets. Or did I?" He gave Emily an inquisitive look, but in a fun way.

"*Nein*," Mary protested, "I just asked where you moved from."

"I told Mary you're looking for a relative," Emily said.

Noah cut his glance from Emily to Mary. "Our parents' families were Amish, and I want to try and find our grandparents."

"What are their names? My *stiefmutter* has lived here all her life, she might know them. If she does, I'll introduce you."

"My father's name was Jeremiah Miller, and my mother was Naomi Knepp."

Mary's face heated, and her hands flew to her hips. "You're a relative of Seth Knepp?" The words snapped out a littler harsher than she'd intended.

Noah finished his cupcake, took Emily's hand and guided her to the door. "Apparently, you and he aren't good friends. But I don't know if he's a relative or not. He could be. Thanks for the cupcakes."

Her heart nearly stuttered to a stop. Had Seth sent them to get to know her and maybe to try and make peace between him and her? A likely story that Noah didn't know where his relatives lived. She might be on the verge of losing business to competition and now a possible relative of Seth visited her shop. Why? Was it just a friendly visit?

As the sting of guilt shimmied up his back, Noah pressed a hand on Emily's shoulder and hurried her across the street to his Farm-fresh Grocery, Delicatessen and Bakery. Mary hadn't mentioned his store, so apparently she hadn't realized who he really was, but she would soon enough.

He liked Mary, but the town was too small to support two bakeries. The pit of his stomach roiled at the thought of what was probably going to happen to her bakery. His store in Iowa City was very successful, and he had every reason to believe it would be equally so here in Kalona.

While he locked the door of his store behind them, Emily took off running toward the office. "I'm going to play games on the computer."

"Okay, but only for an hour, then you can sweep the floor." At the sound of shuffling feet and moving cartons, he turned and found Jenny stocking shelves. He scanned her handiwork. "Looks good."

Jenny finished placing serrated knives on a display stand. "I'm still wondering if this was the right move. This town is so small. What did the baker say when you went to get Emily?"

"I didn't tell her we owned the new store."

"Noah, you coward. You should have been honest."

He took a step back from the impact of her words. "She gave Emily and me a free cupcake and said for you to stop in for yours. I didn't have the heart to tell her right then. You can tell her."

"Thanks a lot." She rolled her eyes.

"Since you're going to attend nursing school in the fall, you won't be here if there's fussing."

She tossed him a disgusted look.

He took a step closer to Jenny. "Why don't you go over there and say hi? Her name is Mary. Since the Amish shunned our parents, we need to make friends in the Plain community before they find out who we are."

Jenny huffed as she set a few baking timers on the shelf. "We don't know that our parents were shunned. We know nothing about what happened after they left their Order. The only thing that's clear is that they left during their *rumspringa*, had a civil wedding and never went back to the faith. They said they didn't want to live by the *Ordnung* and the church rules. They wanted to live like the *Englisch*."

Naoh shrugged. "But you know as well as I do that we didn't live like the *Englisch*. Mom homeschooled us, and we weren't allowed to play or associate with *Englisch* kids at the park. We couldn't go to the movies or hang out with the neighbor kids our age. Our parents might not have wanted to be Amish, but our upbringing was strict and definitely not *Englisch*. And if our parents didn't join the Amish church, they weren't shunned."

Jenny set the last timer on the shelf. "If the community did shun them, maybe we shouldn't have opened a store here." She took a step closer. "And what makes you think that our relatives want to meet us?" She raised a brow, turned and headed toward the office.

He heaved a long sigh. *Sisters.* Jenny would thank him later when she had a grandma to wrap her in a hug and attend her wedding someday… But Jenny was right. He needed to visit them and put the question of what had happened to rest.

Emily slipped out the office door and sprinted to Noah. "I want to help stock shelves."

"Did Jenny chase you off the computer and tell you to help me?" He didn't have time to show an eight-year-old a task and then clean up the mess she made.

Emily tugged at a box and tried to get it open. "Can you help me?"

"Right now we're just unpacking a few things we brought from the other store. The trucks will be here tomorrow with our fresh vegetables. When I get it unpacked, you can help stock the shelves and bins." Noah could see the disappointment in her eyes. He pulled a stack of flyers from behind the counter and handed them to Emily. "Why don't you tape one of these on the shelf by the item they advertise? Then post some of the others around the store so the shoppers can see them."

"I'll do a great job."

He watched Emily hang one on the wall by the entrance. She walked to the first aisle and posted another by the fruit table.

When Noah finished stocking shelves, he checked on Emily and every aisle that had a sale item had a flyer over the correct area. "Good job, Emily."

He headed to the deli area as his mind wandered back to what Jenny said about the Amish. If this was such a strong, Amish-supporting town, it might not be the Amish Sweet Delights driven out of business, but his store.

He shoved his hand into his pocket and pulled out an entry form. The fall festival had scheduled a baking contest with a $10,000 prize. What better advertisement for his bakery than winning a baking contest? His cupcakes were every bit as good as Mary's, if not better.

Mary would probably enter the competition. But if either one of them won, they could capture a lot of the town and tourist business. As a result, it could possibly drive the other out of business. And if that happened, he'd never see those cornflower-blue eyes or her silky blond hair again. He liked her, and he would truly hate never seeing her again.

Chapter Two

Grabbing potholders, Mary opened the oven door letting a steamy whiff of pecan-caramel rolls fill the kitchen. She pulled the pans out, set them on the cooling rack next to the cinnamon rolls and let their aromas mingle.

"Those smell *gut*." Amanda glanced up from rolling dough.

"*Danki*. It has been a busy morning, glad it's slowing down." Mary scooted from the kitchen to the front of the bakery, pulled out the medium roast and decaf bags, and started fresh coffee. She puttered around cleaning the counter, wiping off tables and straightening chairs.

When the front door opened, the aroma of fresh-brewed coffee wafted around the bakery on a cool breeze. Mary noticed a tall, slender young woman enter who looked remarkably like Emily.

Mary eased her way around a table and met the visitor at the counter. "Hallo. Are you Jenny?"

"Yes, I'm Emily and Noah's sister. I wanted to introduce myself." Her gaze roamed around the bakeshop and over the display case full of chocolate cupcakes, sugar cookies, cherry tarts, and a vanilla bean cake with deep swirls of buttercream frosting.

"It's very nice to meet you, Jenny. I'm Mary Brenneman. Pick out anything you like, and it's on the house. My way of saying *willkommen*."

"Thank you, and it's nice to meet you, too." Jenny took a step back and drew in a deep breath. "The strawberry pie smells divine, but I'll take a chocolate chunk cookie to go, please. I'm a cookie freak and choc-o-holic. I like washing down a warm, gooey cookie with a cold glass of milk."

"*Gut* choice. They're my favorite cookie."

"It sounds like there is a cookie break." Amanda walked to the front holding two small ice cream cones. "We are experiment-ing with serving ice cream with our des-serts. It's old fashioned vanilla bean and on the haus." Amanda held out a cone to Jenny and handed the other to Mary.

"Thank you." Jenny licked a drip on the side of the cone. "Mmm, that's very good." She motioned toward the door. "Shall we step outside and eat these? It's a lovely day."

"*Jah*, a breath of fresh air might be nice." Mary opened the door and held it for Jenny. "Are you coming, Amanda?"

"*Nein*. I'll stay and box up the cookies and cupcakes for the fireman's bake sale tomorrow."

Mary leaned against a lamppost and took a lick of her cone. "Emily's a sweet little girl. She told me about your move here from Iowa City. How are you adjusting to small-town life? It's a lot different than the city, *jah*?"

Jenny laughed. "Yes, it's different. Noah wanted to expand the business to Kalona because of the large amount of Amish tourism. The leather-and-wood craft shops, the sewing shops and consignment stores are a big draw for the tourists."

The jingling of harness rings and the clomping of horses' hooves pulled Mary's attention up the street. She straightened her back and gasped. "Is that Noah standing in front of the Farm-fresh Grocery and Deli?"

Jenny followed Mary's gaze. "Yes, but I don't know who the other man is helping him move in that shelving. He's cute."

"That's Ethan Lapp. The new grocery and deli belongs to Noah?" The words exploded from Mary's mouth like a geyser.

"Yes. I'm sorry he forgot to mention it earlier that we own the store. I'm helping Noah set up the computer and bookkeeping system, but I'm only here until I start nursing school next month. He hired a manager to run the store in Iowa City while he dedicated his time here."

"Your *bruder* never mentioned that." Mary gritted her teeth and the words tumbled out a little stiffer than she'd intended. He visited her bakery and never said a word about owning the new store.

Noah and Ethan crossed the street toward Amish Sweet Delights. Noah took his hat off and wiped his brow. "Ethan, this is my sister Jenny." He stood silent a minute as those two seemed to take to each other right away. Noah took a step closer to Mary. "I owe you an apology for not telling you that I owned the new store."

She fumed as agitation streaked through her veins. "Did you visit my bakery to snoop and see how long it would take you to put me out of business?"

"No, of course not. I hope there is plenty of business for both of us."

"You do know it's a small town of less

than five thousand, right? I don't understand how you could think there wouldn't be a problem here." Mary raised her chin, turned abruptly as a strand of hair bounced around her face and headed back into the bakery.

Now she had to win the contest and show Noah that she wasn't going to let him steal her business. Tonight, she'd pull out the recipe book Sarah had given her and look for the perfect apple recipe.

A twinge settled in her stomach. She liked Noah, but this was business. This time she was fighting for what she loved.

The next morning, Mary hitched her buggy and coaxed King into a gentle trot down Fifth Street toward the fire station. She slowed the buggy as it passed Carson's flower shop to gawk at the pots of gorgeous yellow and gold chrysanthemums sitting in the display window. She parked the buggy by the curb between Knit 'n' Sew and the fire station, stepped down and carefully lifted out the box of cookies and cupcakes to donate to the firefighters' annual bake sale. The proceeds would go to help needy families who had lost everything after a fire or natural disaster.

Mary set the box down, pulled out her individual containers of baked goods and neatly arranged them on the sale table. She glanced around at the other donations until her scan stopped at some delicious-looking pastries with Noah's store logo on the boxes: Miller's Farm-fresh Grocery, Delicatessen and Bakery.

Bakery, too! Heat rose from her neck and burned on her cheeks. Her pulse accelerated. So that's why he hadn't wanted to introduce himself. His store was also a bakery…and situated right across the street from Sweet Delights. How had she not noticed that?

Out of the corner of her eye, a firefighter dressed in yellow Nomex gear and clomping boots headed her way. Noah Miller. She turned and watched him hand out deli sandwiches to the other firefighters as he approached.

"Thanks for the donations, Mary." His overly friendly voice rang in her ear.

Mary stepped back and motioned to his gear. "So, there is no end to your talents?"

"I volunteered in Iowa City before we moved here."

"And your grocery and deli is also a bakery?"

He nodded toward his donations on the table and smiled. "Yeah. I'm a good baker, learned the trade from my dad."

The more she saw Noah, the more he annoyed her. "The community is fortunate to have you." She turned, walked back to her buggy, climbed in, snapped the reins and braced herself. King jerked the buggy into motion and skedaddled down the street toward the corral and her bakery.

A few minutes later, Mary slammed Sweet Delights' back door. Amanda jerked away from the sink and nearly lost her balance.

"Sorry, I didn't mean to scare you."

"What's going on? You look upset." This time Amanda braced her back on the sink.

"Go take a look out the front window at the uncovered sign on top of Miller's store."

Amanda hurried to the front and returned. "A bakery, too."

"*Jah.* He donated baked goods to the firefighters' bake sale. When I looked around, he was handing out a stack of sandwiches, apparently samples from his deli for the firefighters. Oh, and he's a volunteer firefighter."

Mary huffed to the sink, washed her hands and whirled around. "Put thick frosting on all the cupcakes today and decorate them extra special. Tomorrow is Noah's grand opening. We are fighting fire with fire! No, make that cupcake with cupcake!"

At 8:00 Friday morning, Mary stomped to the chalkboard and drew a delicious-looking cupcake, piled high with frosting swirls and topped with a fresh strawberry. She added another line with the special for the day— Free cupcake with the purchase of a coffee—then turned the board so the writing was visible from the sidewalk.

She dusted the chalk off her hands then poured a cup of medium roast. Usually, she was so busy in the morning that she didn't get a coffee break until ten o'clock.

"You're generous today," Amanda said, glancing up from sliding the cupcake tray into the display case and nodding toward the chalkboard.

"I'm trying to entice a few people to stop in." Mary walked over to the window and gazed up the street at the long line of customers waiting to get into Miller's Farm-fresh Grocery, Delicatessen and Bakery.

"Mary, you knew business would be slow with Noah's grand opening today."

"Yes, I did expect slow. I just wasn't prepared for no one, and tomorrow all our baked goods will be on sale as day-old."

Amanda picked up the empty tray and started for the kitchen, then stopped. "Why don't you go over to Noah's shop and put in a friendly appearance for his open house?"

"What? I couldn't do that." Mary took a step toward the counter. Her palms turned cold and clammy.

"Yes, you can. Go. He came to your bakery."

"He was spying."

"*Nein.* Go. Right now."

Mary sighed. Why did her friend have to be right?

She drew in a ragged breath, crossed the street and opened the door to the Millers' store and stepped inside, letting her long, navy dress swirl around her legs as she turned abruptly to head down an aisle. The mixed aromas of cinnamon rolls, brewed hazelnut coffee and caramel cappuccino hung in the air. Everyone was busy looking around and no one seemed to notice her.

She strolled through the bakery and glanced at his chocolate eclairs, cakes and cookies that smelled of rich European chocolate. The cherry turnovers and pies oozed with ripe-red juice and looked mouthwatering. She rounded the corner to the hot deli bar and the steamy aroma of minestrone soup was luscious. A cheese pizza warmed under a heater next to hot dogs and brats, and a cheeseburger sizzled on the grill. The cold deli bar had fresh melons and green, crisp lettuce and spinach.

Lastly, she walked between two rows of vibrantly colored carrots, cucumbers, beans, potatoes, cilantro and parsley that looked moist and fresh. It all looked *wunderbaar* and inviting. She caught a glimpse of Noah carrying a bowl of cut melon to the deli bar and ducked around the corner as she headed back to the door.

Now what was she going to do? The bad thing about his store was even she wanted to shop here. But she had better leave before Noah caught sight of her and the last thing she wanted was to talk to him about his wunderbaar store.

Mary hurried back across the street. Since Sweet Delights' business was slow, she sent Amanda home early, but she waited and locked up at three o'clock. Dread tugged at her feet as she forced one foot in front of the other all the way to the corral. She hitched King and set him at a leisurely pace as tears stung her eyes. With one hand on the reins, she pulled a hanky from her quilted bag, blotted her eyes and blew her nose.

She watched field after field and yard after yard pass by. The rain yesterday had brightened the countryside to a dark green. The sweet peas and petunias in the Wallins' yard were brilliant pink, purple and white. Her predicament with the bakery eased back into her mind. Noah's store would no doubt be a favorite in town.

Twenty minutes later, while she fought the tears drenching her cheeks, King turned into their barnyard, headed up the driveway and back to the barn. *Daed* met her at the barn door with a warm smile.

"You're home early today. I'll unhitch King and rub him down." He glanced at her face as she stepped down. "What happened, Mary?"

She swallowed a sob. "The new store had

a very successful grand opening today. On the other hand, Sweet Delights didn't have any customers."

Daed sauntered forward and bent his six-foot-frame over her, a swatch of his graying hair poked out from beneath his hat. He wrapped his strong arms around her and hugged as his straggly beard brushed her chin. She could smell his sweat and feel the moisture clinging to his shirt.

"I'm sorry, Mary, but it's only one day. I'm sure your customers will be back tomorrow. You work too much and needed a rest." His words comforted her, but when she took a step back, she caught the lines creasing his forehead that signaled he was worried too. They couldn't afford to lose the business.

Mary nodded then turned toward the *haus*. Each foot hit the path as if it had a weight tied to it. She opened the kitchen screen door and set her bag on a chair.

Her *stiefmutter*, Sarah, turned her tall frame from the sink, a strand of cinnamon-brown hair bobbing by her temple. "You're home early."

"The Millers' new store had their grand-opening today. Everyone was there."

"Oh, I'm sorry." Mamm opened the gas-powered refrigerator door, poured a glass of lemonade and handed it to Mary. "Sit and rest." She resumed peeling apples at the sink.

Mary took the glass and sipped. "I'm worried the bakery won't survive."

Mamm glanced over her shoulder. "Why?"

"I strolled through Noah Miller's store. His baked goods looked *wunderbaar* and the deli had hotdogs, soups, salad bar and pizzas. Everyone will go there for their morning coffee and lunch."

"*Nein.* It's just new. You'll see."

"I need to win the bakery contest next month at the fall festival so we can expand our menu. We have to start serving breakfast sandwiches and lunch in order to compete with Noah's shop. We need that trophy to show we are the best." Mary's voice quivered.

Sarah paused her apple peeling. "So practice and win. I know you can do it. But I don't think the bishop will let you display a trophy, symbolizing you think you are better than someone else."

"If I win, I'll tell them I don't want the trophy. *Mamm,* will you help me pick out the perfect apple recipe? And give me some pointers on how to heighten the flavors and make them shine through for the judges? In the words of Noah's little sister, so it will taste *wow-wee*?"

"Of course. And if you get too busy at the bakery, your *Aent* Lillia said Cousin Nettie would like to come and work with you."

Mary wrapped her arms around *Mamm* and hugged. Her real *mamm* may have died, but her *stiefmutter* was always there for her. Sarah was sweet and always offered her love and support…but sometimes love couldn't fix everything. It certainly hadn't with Seth.

Saturday morning, Mary hitched King to her buggy. His big brown eyes danced with excitement at the chance to stretch his legs. She straightened her dress and settled back on the black seat of her open buggy. She shook the reins, nudging the steed down the drive, out onto the road and past the white picket fence. King set his own pace and fell into a steady trot.

The scent of wildflowers saturated the breeze and enticed her to draw a deep breath. The fresh fragrance cleared her mind and invigorated her senses.

Sarah was right. Of course, Mary could bake better than Noah. She'd baked all her life. Why hadn't she purchased something from his bakery so she could have sampled his talent? Now it would be awkward if she went back and bought a cupcake. It would look suspicious.

Where the road paralleled the English River, she pulled back on the reins. "Whoa, King, slow down, big guy." She wanted to enjoy the bright blue sky and the birds singing. The sun danced off the river like a thousand jewels just sitting there ready for plucking. Mary didn't often see the sunrise. Usually she was already at work before now, but since the shop had so many baked goods leftover from yesterday, today they wouldn't need to bake as much.

Pulling back on the reins, she steered King to a bare spot and stopped the buggy. Stepping down, she surveyed the riverbank until she spotted what she was looking for, a big rock positioned under a tree. She'd passed this spot hundreds of times and had always wanted to stop. It looked like the perfect place to sit, sort things out and organize her world into order once again.

She eased onto the rock, leaned back against the tree and watched the river flow and babble over rocks. The birds chirping, frogs jumping in the river and the relaxing sounds of nature soothed her mind. Her gaze landed on a leaf caught in the current, barreling down the river. It was the first fall leaf she'd seen, and it reminded her that change was coming—and she'd better get ready. She could no longer sit and do nothing.

The sound of tires crunching over sticks and rocks pulled her attention toward the road as an SUV stopped on the shoulder and parked. Noah Miller climbed out and headed in her direction. What did he want?

Mary scooted to the edge of the rock as she watched him approach. After her breakup with Seth, her life was just starting to return to some kind of normal, until Noah showed up in town.

His purposeful stride carried him to her side in seconds. Just as he stopped next to her, an annoying breeze kicked up, ruffled her apron, tugged a few strands of hair from her prayer *kapp* and tapped it against her cheek. And her day was only starting.

After choosing the shortest route over tall weeds to Mary's rock, Noah slowed his pace when he reached the clearing. The glimpse of her perched beside the river framed by shrubs and trees filled him with a smile. "Are you okay, Mary? Did your buggy break down?"

She jerked her head around at his remark. "I'm fine. The river just looked so peaceful this morning it beckoned me to stop. I enjoy a quiet spot." Her gaze swept over him before she turned toward the river. "Thanks for stopping."

"I saw you at the grand opening, what did you think?" He wasn't going to let her off that easily. He wanted to talk to her whether she liked it or not.

"I was merely putting in an appearance to pay my respects to a new shop opening. I wasn't there long, but it looked like you had a nice turnout."

"Okay, but what did you think?"

She kept her back to him. "It's nice, but I'm a better baker, Noah." She said teasingly."

"Is that right?" He took a step back.

"That's right" came a smug goading reply.

"Well, Miss Brenneman, I'm entering the fall festival baking contest. Are you?"

She jumped to her feet, whirled around to face him and lifted her chin. "Yes."

"Good. Game on. Let the best baker win." He laughed. She was sassy, but he wanted to pull her and that cute attitude into his arms. But the fear of looking like a complete and utter fool kept him away.

"You make it sound like a kid's game." She said the last word with a pout before she flattened her full lips into a straight line.

Noah started to leave, then stopped. "We both know there's much more at stake here than merely winning a contest. At this point, it's not even the money, is it? It's the title, the trophy and the prestige that goes along with the achievement."

"As usual, Noah, you've thought of it all." Her eyes challenged his.

He took a step closer. "I'm surprised your bishop would actually allow you to enter. It's such an open display of pride that you think your baking is so good you could actually win a contest."

The surprise that covered her face told him she hadn't thought about asking the bishop or the church for approval to enter the contest. It would be interesting to see how she maneuvered around that obstacle.

Without another word, he turned and tromped back to his car. A chuckle shook his body as he opened the door and sat. Yeah, this was not only going to be a game of skill, but one of wit.

He'd tasted Mary's cupcakes. They were delicious, but his parents had trained him well in how to run their store and how to bake. He was a better baker than Jenny. That was the reason she took care of the books, and he baked and ran the store. He had a knack for figuring out what flavors complemented each other. And he might even be a better baker than Mary Brenneman.

At twenty years old, Noah didn't have much experience with women. He'd never taken a girl out to the movies or ball games like most *Englisch* boys had. But he'd met a few women at the store, and they'd gone to lunch together. Most of them wore heavy makeup, short dresses or tight jeans. They flirted and pouted with red lips when he didn't ask them out for more than lunch. Many of them had been attractive, yet none had interested him. Mary was different. She was natural and beautiful.

Noah glanced back at the river and at her sitting on the rock again. He'd asked her about his opening only because he'd wanted to stay and talk to her. The notion to tease her about the contest had just popped out, and it had gone a little further than he had planned. Now, in hindsight, he saw her point of view. His new business was taking some of her customers. To her, it wasn't a tease.

One thing was for sure and certain, as his *mamm* would have said, he might have just made her angry enough to search for days to find that perfect recipe to beat him.

Chapter Three

Mary jumped to her feet as Noah drove away from the river. Tears sprang to her eyes. Surely the bishop and the Gmay, the church members, wouldn't deny her this opportunity. Would they? Could they?

Nein, she hadn't considered that. She participated last year, but they only paid the winner $200 then. This year, they were trying to attract more festivalgoers so they increased the prize money.

She raced to her buggy. Her hands shaking as she picked up the reins and set King to a smart pace. The buggy rocked as he lengthened his gait. A mile down the road,

Mary turned into Bishop Yoder's drive, parked and hurried to his front porch.

She hesitated at the door. It was early, maybe too early to pay the bishop a visit. She drew in a deep breath, blew it out and knocked.

After a few seconds, the door opened and Mrs. Yoder stared at her with a surprised look on her face. "*Gut Morgen,* Mary." Rebecca waved her in. "You're an early bird this morning."

"Mornin', Rebecca. Would it be possible to see the bishop? It's important."

"Of course. Wait right here." The stout woman gave her a peculiar survey before hurrying down the hallway off the vestibule.

Mary inhaled a deep whiff of fresh-brewed coffee as she pressed her right hand to her heart to slow its runaway drumming. The last time she'd visited the bishop's farm was a year ago when she had to inform him that Seth had canceled their wedding.

Bishop Yoder appeared at his office door. He nodded at his *frau* and headed toward

Mary, his hair a bit mussed, as if he hadn't planned on a visitor this early.

"*Gut Morgen*, Mary. It must be important for you to interrupt my prayer time." His words were to the point but softly spoken.

"I'm so sorry. I didn't think about the time. I was on my way to work, but I can come back." Heat rose to her cheeks as she turned toward the door.

"*Nein, nein.* I'm up. We can talk. Come." He led the way down the hall to his office, motioned for her to go in, then stuck his head into the kitchen across the hall. "Rebecca, would you please bring us two cups of coffee?"

The room was small, cool and sparsely decorated with only a desk and three chairs, counting his. She sat in a hard wooden chair in front of his desk and waited for the bishop to give her a sign to start talking. He talked about the weather and asked about her family.

Rebecca knocked. After his reply, she set the tray on his desk and closed the door. He motioned for Mary to grab a cup. "Now, what is this all about?"

She took a sip and set the cup back on the tray. "I want to enter the fall festival baking contest and compete for the $10,000 prize." She blurted out as a nudge of excitement loosened her tongue.

The bishop's eyes widened. "Mary, our belief is that we live in community and give up personal expression. The *Ordnung* calls us to live in submission to God's will. We live in harmony with the others in our community. We do not *compete* for who is best."

His words speared her heart. Mary straightened her back as her old rebellious nature clutched her. "Bishop, the bakery is our livelihood. *Daed* and *Mamm* have medical bills from the twins' birth that we do not burden the community with. We pay from Sweet Delights' revenue."

"*Jah*, I understand. But we do not seek acclaim for what we do. We strive for a godly life to attain eternal salvation."

Mary sat forward on the chair and squared

her shoulders. "I am not doing it to brag or boast. In fact, I have very little chance of even winning. Many who enter the contest will have gone to culinary school, like the winner of the contest last year. With the new grocery opening across the street, our bakery has already lost business. This is no different from offering a loaf of bread for sale. I make it, and if they like it, they purchase it. I need to compete with other businesses, and to do that, I need to expand our menu. In order to do that, I need the prize money."

The bishop rubbed his hand down his beard as he directed his gaze toward the ceiling.

Leaning back, Mary gripped the arms of the hard, wooden chair. The longer he took, the more her pulse increased and the further her heart sank.

Bishop Yoder lowered his gaze to her. "*Jah*, it would appear that you have the same right to offer your product, but this is highly unusual. Accepting the money for a recipe is one thing, but you must not accept a trophy.

And the other ministers may want to discuss it, but we will see. I'll let you know. Now, Rebecca will have my breakfast ready." He stood, motioned toward the door and followed her down the hall to the entrance.

Heading out of the *haus*, Mary blew out a deep sigh. She climbed in the buggy and relaxed back against the seat for her ride to Sweet Delights. She unhitched King, led him to the corral and hurried to the back door.

As she approached, a light shining out a high window caught her attention. Had she left the light on yesterday when she went home? *Nein*, she always walked through her routine. Her keys jangled as she unlocked Sweet Delights' back door. She drew in a deep breath of humid Iowa August air. She pushed the door slowly open and peeked in.

She laughed at the sight of her assistant and then stepped into an atmosphere scented with medium-roast hazelnut brewing. "You're in early, Amanda."

"Couldn't sleep." Amanda yawned and

clasped an elbow over her mouth for a second. "Coffee is almost ready."

"*Danki*, I could use some. I had to stop by Bishop Yoder's *haus* and ask if I could enter the baking contest. He's going to let me know." Mary stowed her quilted bag in the closet and grabbed the ingredients for a batch of sugar cookies.

Within a few minutes, she was popping them in the oven and starting on the chocolate chip batch. Amanda's yeast bread and rolls cooling on the counter sent warm, steamy whiffs of honey and cinnamon into the air.

"You're in early, too. Couldn't sleep? Thinking about Noah's bakery or Noah?" Amanda teased.

"Neither." That man infuriated her. "After Seth ran off to go live with the *Englisch*, I just want to avoid men, especially if they are *Englisch*. They can't be trusted. I thought I knew Seth, knew what he wanted. I thought he wanted me. I was blind." *Jah*, he talked about the *Englisch* world and wanting to be able to do whatever he wanted with no rules to restrict him. But she'd thought it was just talk. When Seth asked her to go with him and she said *nein*, he'd strolled out of her *haus* and out of her life…forever.

Amanda pulled a pan of tea biscuits from the oven and set them to cool. "We both are *gut* bakers, but we have terrible taste in men. I've always liked Ethan Lapp, but he doesn't know I exist, at least not anymore. When Ethan and I were younger, we were neighbors, grew up together, went fishing and palled around together every chance we got. I guess my feelings grew and his didn't. Now whenever he's in the bakery, he just asks me about Jenny. He asked me if I knew if she had a boyfriend. I've seen him talking to her."

"I'm sorry, Amanda. Do you want me to casually let it drop to Ethan that you like him?"

"*Nein*, but *danki* for the offer.

"You, my friend, are a lovely slim redhead, and a great baker. You'll find your

Mr. *Wunderbaar*. He'll come along when you least expect it and sweep you away from my bakery."

"*Danki*. You are sweet to say that."

Mary tucked her broken engagement in the attic of her mind and slammed the door closed. "I have news. There is no chance Noah and I will become friends. He told me this *morgen* that he's entering the fall baking contest. He's planning on winning, taking the prize and getting all the benefits, meaning customers. He is now a rival."

Amanda gasped. "Don't worry, you'll win."

"*Jah*, I'll try to find the perfect recipes." Mary pulled her cookies from the oven while her mind wandered back to Noah at the river. She hated to admit it, but it was nice of him to stop and see if she had a problem.

Amanda pushed the cart up to the counter. "Ready to load?"

"Yes, *danki*, time got away from me." Mary helped Amanda pile the cart with rolls, bread and cookies, laughing like two young girls as they filled the display case.

At 7:00 a.m., Mary pulled the dead bolt back and flipped the sign to Open. Before she reached the counter, Carolyn Ropp pushed the door open, bumping her Miller's Farm-fresh Grocery bag against the door-jamb.

"*Morgen*, Mary." She sighed. "I'll sure be glad when canning season is over so I can get some rest. A loaf of wheat bread, please."

Mary picked up a loaf and turned to Carolyn. "Did you say one or two loaves?"

"Just one."

"Last week you got two." Mary bagged the loaf and set it on the counter.

Carolyn's face turned a bright red as she fished the money out of her purse. "I stopped at the grocery across the street. His bread looked so *gut* that I just had to try one."

"Of course, I understand." Heat engulfed Mary's chest. She pushed her mouth into a smile as Carolyn whirled around and headed toward the door.

Frank Wallin held the door open as Carolyn hustled out. He raised his brow at her abrupt exit but nodded a greeting and headed for the counter. "Good morning, Mary. I'll take my usual."

She nodded and prepared his order. "I haven't seen you for a couple of days, Frank, been running late?"

"Ah, yeah...running late." Taking his breakfast, he laid down his money. "No change." He hastily turned and headed for the door.

Amanda poked her head out of the kitchen. "See, your customers are loyal. They just visited Noah's store because it was his grand opening."

Mary walked across the bakery, glanced out the window and noticed some of her other customers walking on the sidewalk, carrying paper bags with Noah's logo.

"Maybe, we'll see." The pit of her stomach flipped like a rubbery pancake. She returned to the counter just as Emily heaved the door open and jumped aside as it swept back closed.

"Good morning, Emily. What can I get you today?"

"I don't have any money. I just wanted to say hi. I was bored watching Noah stock shelves."

"You're not helping?"

"He says it takes too long to tell me what to do when he can have it done in the time it takes to show me." A lingering hint of hurt feelings pushed out the last few words.

"Well, I'm sure he's trying to get the store restocked quickly. Tell you what, wash your hands, and you can help Amanda and me make cookies."

"Okay!" Emily turned toward the washroom then stopped. "I heard Noah tell Jenny this morning that if nothing else, you're a good baker."

Mary jerked her head around. "Is that so?"

"Yeah. He also said you're heavy-handed, and he said that meant you made your cookies and cupcakes really big so you can charge more."

Mary watched Emily disappear behind the washroom door. Was that right? If nothing else…she was a *gut* baker but heavy-handed. He had his nerve saying that.

The Lord nudged her heart at her uncharitable thoughts toward Noah.

Emily held her hands up as she entered the kitchen. "All clean."

"Very nice." Mary handed Emily a cookie scooper. "Please drop walnut-size peanut butter cookies onto the baking sheet. After you're finished, I'll show you how to sugar and flatten them."

Emily measured the dough out to precisely the size of a walnut and dropped it on the cookie sheet. "I like making cookies."

"You do a very *gut* job, little one," Amanda cooed.

Mary buttered the bottom of another pan. "When do you start school?"

"My first full day is the twenty-sixth. I'm scared though. Mom homeschooled me, but

Jenny and Noah said they don't have time this year."

"You'll like it. You'll meet all the other kids in town, and you'll find some nice friends."

When the doorbell jingled, Mary hurried to the front of the bakery. "*Morgen*, Cyrus."

"*Gut Morgen*. Nice to see you, Mary. My frau is still canning and would like two loaves of whole wheat bread."

She bagged the bread and handed the sack across the counter to Cyrus, but he was staring off toward the kitchen with his jaw dropped open. Mary followed his gaze.

Emily stood in the kitchen doorway quiet as a rabbit. "Mary, I got all the dough dropped onto the cookie sheet."

"*Danki*, sweetie. Why don't you wash the dishes you used? I'll be there in a minute."

Cyrus waited until Emily disappeared into the kitchen and then whispered, "Who is that?"

"Emily Miller."

"She looks familiar, but I can't place her. Whose *tochter*?"

"Her parents are dead. She's the sister of the new owner of Miller's Farm-fresh Grocery, Delicatessen and Bakery across the street. He's *Englisch* but his parents left the community during their *rumspringa*."

"*Englisch*, you say."

"*Jah*. Is something wrong?"

"*Nein*. She just looked familiar."

After Cyrus left, Mary placed a glass and bowl of sugar in front of Emily and demonstrated how to press and sugar the cookies. "Okay, your turn."

Emily picked up the glass, dipped the bottom in sugar, then pressed it gently against the cookie dough.

Mary patted her on the shoulder. "That looks great. They are the perfect size cookies. Honey, did you know that man that was just in the bakery?"

"No. Should I know him? He could have seen me at the store."

"*Jah*, he just thought you looked familiar."

"Maybe he could be the relative Noah is looking for?"

When Emily had the cookie sheet filled, Mary slid it in the oven. "I don't know, but don't worry about it. Noah will find who he is looking for." Only Cyrus Miller and his family were very strict Old Order Amish, and she knew they didn't mix with the *Englisch*. If they were the relatives Noah was looking for, it would be interesting to see how they accepted Noah and his family.

The heavy aroma of buttered breads and rolls, frosted cakes and rhubarb pies hit Noah the second he opened the door to Sweet Delights. When he moved closer to the counter, he smelled cinnamon-spiced coffee—the flavor of the day according to Saturday's chalkboard.

Mary swiped her hands across her apron as she headed to the front of the bakery. Her step slowed when she saw Noah. *"Hallo."*

"Would Emily happen to be here?" His voice wavered as he approached the counter.

He wasn't quite sure how she'd greet him after their confrontation at the river, but he wanted to make sure there wasn't rift between them.

"*Jah*, she's helping Amanda and me bake cookies. Can she stay a while longer so she can finish?"

"Sure, I just don't want her to be a burden."

Mary winced. "*Nein*, we *liebe* having her help and enjoy teaching her to bake. She is a *gut* student."

"I know, it's just that sometimes she's overly helpful. She doesn't have any playmates, so she gets bored." He pushed his hands in his jean pockets and hooked his thumbs over the top.

"I understand." Mary nodded. "But she's doing a *gut* job helping us with baking."

"Thanks for showing her how to bake. I really appreciate it." Noah glanced at the pastry display case, then back at Mary. "Emily wanted to help me earlier when I stocked shelves, and I think I hurt her feelings. I tried to explain how to arrange the inventory, but she pushed everything together on a shelf at her level." Guilt pricked at his heart as he forced the words from his mouth.

Mary nodded knowingly.

He pulled a hand from his pocket and gestured toward Mary. "I know what you're thinking, that she's small and that's what makes sense to her, but I can't have the store shelves looking like that. And it takes me twice as long to straighten out what she did as opposed to just doing it myself. But I have a job lined up for her this afternoon."

Mary flashed him a reassuring smile. "She'll like that. She wants to be helpful. But send her over any time. We like having her company. There's always something she can do here in the bakery, and she's very entertaining." She raised a brow.

He wasn't quite sure now exactly what she meant by *entertaining*. Sometimes Emily repeated things that you hadn't even realized she had overheard. He tried to read Mary's face but her expression covered any other telltale hints.

Noah glanced around. "How long have you had this shop?"

"The bakery belonged to my *stiefmutter*. She had it for several years. Her *vater* started it, and when he died, she took over. A few years ago, she married my *daed*, and now she has three small *kinner*, so I've been managing it for the last three years."

"It looks like you're doing a great job."

"Danki. Cyrus Miller was in the bakery today and saw Emily. He asked her name and thought she look familiar. Do you know Cyrus?"

"No. Do you think he might be a relative of ours?"

"I'll ask *Mamm* if she knew your parents. Cyrus may be a relative, but there are a lot of Millers in the area."

"Oh, I get it now. Are you trying to shake me up, Mary? Are you saying I'm Amish and you want me to have to ask the bishop's permission to enter the baking contest, too?" He chuckled. "By the way, did he give his approval?"

"Ha! You'll have to wait until the contest to find out." The doorbell jingled and Mary turned to the counter. "Have a *gut* day, Noah."

Emily drifted through the kitchen doorway like a butterfly riding the breeze. She fluttered to Noah's side and stopped. "Mary and Amanda let me help make cookies." She held up a clear plastic baggie. "I got to keep these."

He could see how proud she was of herself. "They look good. I heard you were a big help. I have bins assembled at the store, and I'd sure appreciate it if you could fill them with kitchen supplies."

"Okay, but I want to come back again and help Mary sometime."

"If she doesn't mind, it's fine with me." He caught Mary's nod as he started for the door.

At least he and Mary were still on speaking terms. Well, for the present anyway. In a few weeks when the baking competition started, that might all change.

Chapter Four

The next Monday, Noah drove to Iowa City to help Sidney, his assistant, make the baked goods and supervise the seven kitchen staff at the preparation of food for both stores. For the time being, each day one of them would bring the food to Kalona and oversee the deli from 11:00 until 1:00. Right now, it was easier to carry the baked goods and deli food to Kalona until he could determine how much business and additional help he would need.

He jumped out of his SUV and grabbed the cartons from the backseat that he'd use to transport the baked goods back to Kalona. "Morning, Sidney."

"Morning boss. How are things going at the other store? Summer festivals are keeping me busy here."

Noah glanced at his assistant and nodded. He really liked Sidney, but the man could talk you to death if you let him. "It's going good. Each day, more locals stop in, so I think it's going to work out and the branching-out was a good investment. But time will tell."

Pulling flour and yeast from the pantry, Noah started the family-secret bread and roll recipes. It wasn't that he didn't trust Sidney, but the old family recipes were mostly kept in his head. There was a recipe book. His great-grandfather handed it down to his father, and he inherited it. But he kept it locked in the safe.

Noah mixed the ingredients, added the yeast and milk mixture, turned the dough onto a floured board and began to knead. He turned the soft mass and kneaded again.

He plopped the dough in a bowl and pushed it to the corner to rise.

He reached into his memory and pulled out one of the old pie recipes from the book to try for the baking contest. He opened a bag of apples, cored and peeled them and made a piecrust. He mixed the cinnamon topping and sprinkled it on the pie. When he pulled it out of the oven, it looked perfect. He cut a piece and handed it to Sidney.

"Boss, this pie is a winner." He then proceeded to tell Noah about the breakup with his girlfriend, a festival he'd attended, baking and decorating cupcakes for his church's bake sale, all before Noah had finished baking and boxing his products to take back to Kalona.

The quiet trip back to the other store was a welcome change to a morning of listening to Sidney's chatter. The tall green corn waved in the breeze as Noah passed by field after field. Some farmers were combining oats and hauling it to silos. Bits and pieces of chaff blew across the road and lightly dusted his windshield. Now he'd need to add an auto wash to his list of things to do. He parked behind his Kalona store, carried in three cartons of baked goods, unpacked them and arranged the pastries in the display case.

When he finished, he glanced at the closed office door where Jenny was still working on the books and setting up the new computer system.

It was risky opening a new store in such a small town. Especially since he'd heard that Sweet Delights was a tourist favorite. Could this town generate enough business to justify two bakeries?

But one good thing about the move to Kalona, he got to meet Mary Brenneman. An image of her fought its way into his mind. He squeezed his eyes shut and tried to block it out.

He couldn't do it. He didn't really want to do it.

But haunting thoughts of how he was complicating her life shrouded his view.

"Noah."

He jerked around and faced Jenny.

"Would you please take this stack of store flyers to the post office?" He frowned at her orders as she plowed on. "And on your way back, stop at Sweet Delights and bring Emily home. Supper is going to be early tonight because I have a church meeting. By the way, how long do you think it'll be before you can handle the store on your own?"

He drew a steadying breath. "I'll never be able to do all the work by myself. I can run the store, but I'll still need you to manage the office and do the bookkeeping. We should continue to run the business like Mom and Dad did."

One glance at her face told him that wasn't a good enough answer.

He paced the floor in front of Jenny. "I don't have the cash to hire someone to replace you right now. The move to expand the business was expensive."

"I've received a student loan, and I've signed up for nursing classes that start in

September. You can have my share of the profits from the store in Iowa City to pay for your help. Remember, this move to expand was your idea. You were the one who wanted to chase down family members, who, by the way, have never seen us and probably don't want anything to do with us. This is your dream, and mine is nursing. I love you, Noah, but I want to live my own life, and that life is not here in Kalona."

He held up his hands. "You're right. I know I've been fighting you on this, but I want you to follow your dream."

She blew out a loud sigh. "Is Emily spending too much time at Sweet Delights? They're probably getting sick of her hanging around. I don't want her to be a bother to Mary and Amanda."

"Mary assured me Emily isn't a bother." He huffed through gritted teeth. "She's a little girl who lives above a store in the middle of town. She's new here and has no friends. And we don't have much time to spend with her since the folks died."

"Do you still want to send her to public school this fall? You could hire more help that would free up some time so you could help her with studies." Jenny's voice softened.

He saw where this was going. "She needs friends. And neither of us has the time to homeschool her, especially if you're attending school."

She nodded. "I need to get supper in the oven. After you stop at the post office, don't forget Emily. Supper will be ready in thirty minutes."

Noah grabbed his brimmed hat, screwed it down on his head and stepped out the door into a gust of wind. He glanced at the wall of dark clouds rolling in from the west, ran the one block up Fifth Street to the post office, mailed the flyers, crossed the street and hurried back down Fifth Street to Sweet Delights.

Windblown and slightly wet, he ducked into the bakery and met Mary's gaze as she looked up from wiping the counter. "Good afternoon. I'm here to get Emily." His heart jumped at the sight of that lovely face.

"*Jah*, she has been a great help this afternoon." He watched her eyes twinkle and wondered if it was all for Emily, or maybe just a little bit was for him.

Emily poked her head around the kitchen doorway. "Hi, Noah. I'll be done helping Amanda in a minute."

"Hurry, Jenny has supper ready."

"Just one minute." She held up her index finger.

His attention flicked back to Mary as his thundering heart began to quiet. "How's the entry for the contest coming along?"

"That's off-limits, Noah, I'm not saying a word about my entry."

He laughed. "I'm just making small talk." He turned toward the kitchen door. "Emily, come on we need to get going."

His sister appeared holding a box with a cellophane top showing three chocolate cupcakes inside. She held them up. "I made these all by myself. There were six but we ate three. Amanda said they were delicious." Emily's face beamed with pride.

He glanced at Mary, who smiled and nodded. "They look really good, sis. Tell Mary thanks, we need to go."

"Thanks, Mary." Emily raised her voice. "Thanks, Amanda."

"*Jah*, any time," came the voice from the kitchen.

As Noah headed for the door, a clap of thunder rumbled across the sky. "We better hurry."

He caught Emily's hand, pulled her under Sweet Delights' awning and watched the traffic for a good time to run. When the coast was clear, he rushed her across the street.

As they jumped the curb, sizzling streaks of lightning pierced the sky followed by a long haunting blast from the storm siren. When drops of rain pelted his face, Noah yanked the door open, pushed Emily into the store and jumped in right behind her. A strange tingle twisted in his gut. Whenever he heard a siren, it seemed disaster wasn't far behind. He'd heard that same sound shortly after his folks had left the house the night they'd been killed in a car accident.

He mouthed a silent prayer no one would be hurt this time.

While Amanda waited for her daed to pick her up at Sweet Delights, Mary scanned the ominous sky as she hurried to the corral and hitched King. He shook his head, snorted and pawed the ground. She patted his nose. "*Jah*, I can see you're nervous. Quit acting like that. You're scaring me."

She climbed in the buggy and tapped the reins against King's back. He bolted down the street as if sensing danger. The horse lengthened his gait to a full gallop. "Whoa, King." She pulled back on the reins. He didn't obey. Lightning streaked over their heads and hit the ground close by, causing sparks to fly. She could smell something burning. Wood? Maybe hay. She wasn't quite sure. A boom of thunder sent King galloping even faster.

Mary gripped the reins and pushed back firmly against the seat for whatever was going to happen. She had no control over King. He sensed danger, and so did she. They needed to get off the road but home was three miles away. Surely, they could make it.

Her heart banged against her ribs so hard she thought it would explode. Rain pounded the buggy roof and slashed against the side. When the wheels hit a rut, they slid this way and that. But nothing was slowing King down. Mary bit her bottom lip. If she screamed, the horse would panic.

Stay calm...stay calm...stay calm.

They neared the turnoff to the gravel road, but King was still at full gallop. "Whoa, King, whoa." Panic raced through every fiber of her being. "King, whoa!"

King knew the road and every blade of grass from here to the farm. He knew where his home was, and he wanted to be in his barn eating his oats. King ignored Mary's tugging on the reins. He turned off the asphalt onto the country road at nearly a full gallop. When he turned left, the buggy slid right, jerking King from his footing and pulling him down into the ditch.

The buggy swayed, the door flopped open and a cracking noise filled Mary's ears before something very, very hard hit her...

Noah trudged up the stairs wiping rain from his face and following Emily to their living quarters. As usual, Jenny was prompt. The table was set, a chicken vegetable casserole and Dutch slaw sat waiting in the middle while she poured lemonade.

"Sit—" Jenny gestured toward the chairs "—before the bread dries out." She placed the lemonade on the table and sat before Noah said the blessing.

He watched Jenny dish casserole onto Emily's plate and reach for his. "Oh, no! Don't fill my plate yet." He jumped from his chair.

"What's wrong?" Jenny's hand clutched her throat.

"I forgot to tell Mary to ask her *mamm* if she knew our grandparents, and if so, where they lived. I'll just run over there and be right back."

He ran down the stairs, snatched his hat on the way out the door, dashed across the street and shoved the bakery door open.

Amanda jumped back from the counter. "*Ach,* you scared me."

"Sorry. Can I talk to Mary?"

"It looked bad out, so she hitched King and headed home."

"She didn't wait it out here?"

"*Nein.* She thought the rain looked like it was in for all night, so she wanted to try to get home before it started. I told her I'd lock up since daed is picking me up, and we only live on the edge of town."

The storm sirens roared to life again. Noah looked at Amanda. "That's the second time tonight they've gone off."

She nodded. "Now you have me worried

about Mary, but she only lives three miles away. Maybe she made it home. It would only take a few minutes."

"Can you tell me where she lives? I want to make sure she got home."

"Well..." she glanced toward the window "...okay."

Amanda rattled off the directions. He nodded, tore out of the bakery and headed to the alley where he parked his SUV.

Noah's hand was shaking as he put the vehicle in gear. If she wasn't stranded along the side of the road, should he pull in her driveway and knock on the door to make sure she'd made it home? But if her dad answered the door, would he wonder why an Englischer was there to see Mary? He wouldn't want to get her into any trouble. Yet he had to make sure she was safe. And maybe he could meet her *mamm* and ask if she knew his family.

He turned off the asphalt onto the gravel road. A triangle reflector, the kind on the backs of Amish buggies, caught his eye, and then he saw the buggy lying in the ditch. Nearby, a horse was trying to get up from the ground.

Noah parked just off the road, grabbed his flashlight out of the glove box, said a prayer and hurried to the accident. He swept the light back and forth. "Mary?"

The knot in his throat made it hard to swallow, and his stomach wanted to heave. The buggy's axle looked like it was broken and a wheel had slid off. "Mary, are you here?" The buggy door was open.

He listened. The horse raised his head and whinnied.

He had to find Mary. He flashed the beam all around on the ground. Carefully, he lifted the wheel and the beam danced across her white apron. He quickly set the wheel off to the side, clear of Mary.

She moved her head slowly and moaned. Water dripped off her cheek as Noah knelt next to her. "Are you hurt?"

"No," she said softly. "Nothing is broken. When the buggy veered into the ditch, the door unlatched. I fell out. I guess I got the wind knocked out of me when I hit the ground or when the wheel hit me."

"If you can walk, I'll put you in my SUV and take you to your farm."

She huffed out an exasperated breath. "*Nein*, I'll wait here. I'm sure *Daed* will be along shortly looking for me."

"I'm not leaving you out here in the storm. I'll take you home." He grasped her by the shoulders and pulled her up. "How do you feel?"

"A little dizzy, but I can walk."

Slipping an arm around her waist, he helped her onto the seat as her long, wet dress snagged on the door handle. He untangled the material and ran around to the driver's side. "Long dresses are a nuisance, why do you wear them?"

"It's a mile down this road," she said, "first place on the right."

He started the vehicle. "I'll have you home in a few minutes."

"Why are you out here in the country?"

He glanced her way. "I was concerned about you driving in this weather."

She nodded. "You asked why I wear a long dress. To be Amish means to practice the Amish ways at all times. We live our lives according to the *Ordnung*, which is the application of scriptural principles. It's the rules we live by, dress by and carry out *Gott*'s will for our lives. Some *Englisch* have tried to join our church, but many have trouble living according to what Scripture instructs."

Noah raised a brow. "I'm not sure I could do it either." He turned into the driveway and parked by the house. "I'll help you out."

She opened the door but waited until he got there. He slid his arm around her waist and steadied her as she walked to the house. Her *mamm* and *daed* flew out the door onto the porch and helped Mary into the kitchen.

"What happened, where is your buggy and King?" her *daed* asked, moving his attention from Mary to scan Noah with a scrutinizing gaze.

Mary sat on the chair that her *bruder* had pulled away from the table. "King was spooked by the lightning and thunder, and I couldn't get him to slow down. He took the turn onto the gravel road too fast, the buggy slid in the ditch, the axle broke and the wheel fell off. King wasn't hurt. Noah came along in his SUV, found me and brought me home. This is Noah Miller." She nodded in his direction. "This is my *stiefmutter* Sarah, my *daed* Caleb, my *bruder* Jacob, and this is my munchkin four-year-old *bruder* Michael Paul. And my *boppli* one-year-old twin sisters are probably in bed."

"I'm not a munchkin, sis," Michael protested. "I'm big. I help *Daed* with chores and milking." He wrapped his hands through his suspenders and stretched them.

"*Mamm*, Noah is the new store owner, well, him and his two sisters Jenny and Emily." She paused and rubbed her shoulder. "He's trying to find their grandparents. His *daed* was Jeremiah Miller and his *mamm* was Naomi Knepp."

Sarah glanced at Noah. "*Jah*, I knew your *mamm* and *daed*. I was sorry to see them leave. Jeremiah's parents are Anna and Thomas Miller. Your father's *bruders* are Cyrus and Jonah, and he has a *schwester*, Judith. Your *mamm*'s parents were Enos and Susan Knepp, but they have passed on. They had two other children, Carl and Lydia."

Caleb motioned to his son. "Jacob, we better go see to King and the buggy. We need to at least get him home."

"I can help you, Caleb." Noah started toward the door.

"*Danki*, but Jacob and I can manage the horse. If the axle is broken, we'll wait until the *morgen* to fix that."

Sarah nodded. "*Danki* for bringing Mary home." Her voice held a cool air as if it was a strange thing to say to an *Englischer*.

"*Danki* for helping me home, Noah." Mary slumped back in the chair, her eyelids almost closed.

They were polite, but it was a cool welcome. *Jah*, he got the hint. They were as uncomfortable with an *Englischer* in their *haus* as he was to be there. It was unlikely he'd be asked back. He touched the brim of his hat and nodded to Mary and her mother. He opened the screen door, stepped onto the porch, but the stiff spring banged the door close. Yeah, he got it. They closed the door between him and Mary.

Chapter Five

Mary stared out the kitchen window into the rainy evening until Noah drove out of sight. A smile tugged at the corners of her mouth at the thought of his warm amber eyes. He had a charming way about him. But he was chasing the same prize she was, and there could only be one winner.

"How did he happen along in the rain to help you home? Doesn't he live in town?" Her stiefmutter startled Mary out of her muse.

"Amanda told him I had headed home. We talk occasionally. Since it was storming, he thought he'd better make sure I'd arrived safely."

Sarah raised a brow. "Noah's *grossdaddi* Thomas is a quiet man, and it hurt him deeply when Jeremiah and Naomi left and never came back. I've been told Thomas is strict and doesn't mingle with the *Englisch*, so I'm not sure how he'll accept Noah and his sisters."

Mary moved her sore shoulder and winced. "If he doesn't want to be part of their lives, that'll hurt Noah's feelings. I don't know Thomas well, but his *frau*, Anna, is very nice." Mary cast a long look at the door Noah had gone through. She was almost sorry they were in competition for the same prize. But the fact remained... they were.

"*Mamm*, I need a recipe that'll charm the judges' taste buds. Old Bishop Ropp was in the bakery the other day and talked about an apple pie recipe that your *daed* made. He said he'd drive five miles for a piece. Do you remember the recipe?"

"*Nein*, but after supper, I'll dig in the

boxes of stuff in storage and see if I can find his recipe book."

When the last clean dish sat in the cupboard, Mary followed Sarah to the attic. She dug in one box while *Mamm* unloaded another old carton but nothing turned up resembling a recipe book.

"I'm going back to the bakery tomorrow. I'll search through the recipe books there again. One of them has to be it."

"*Nein*, Mary, you should rest at least a couple of days after your accident."

"*Mamm*, I'm fine. I can't leave Amanda alone to do all the baking."

The truth was…she also wanted to see Noah.

Wednesday morning, Mary hurried around Sweet Delights packing three cartons with pastries, breads and cookies. She carted them to her buggy, or rather Mamm's buggy since hers wasn't fixed yet. She and Amanda had worked hard getting the food ready to contribute to today's barn raising.

News had quickly spread that Noah's *gross-daddi*'s barn had burned to the ground after a lightning strike. But the Plain folk would have a new one built in no time.

From barn-raising flyers posted everywhere, Noah would probably be there too. And she liked the idea of seeing him again. His tall, broad-shouldered frame and amber eyes flashed through her brain. Jah, he was sure cute.

After the four-mile trip, Mary turned King up Thomas Miller's drive and parked at the end of the long row of buggies. Glancing around the barnyard, there must have been a hundred men working who had already raised the outer four walls. Some men were sawing lumber, others nailing while the young climbed to the top of the structure. Ladders, hammers and saws were all busy.

Jah, she'd better hurry, the men would be hungry and thirsty after all that hard work.

The women were gathering in the yard at the long tables they used for the Sunday common meal and were setting out food. Mary carried her cartons across the yard to the tables and set them at one end. She laid out her pastries, breads and desserts, then noticed a group of women gathering at the other end of the table. Friends and women she hadn't seen in a while were talking and no doubt sharing their news and gossip.

Anna Miller, Thomas's *frau*, walked out onto the porch, glanced Mary's way and gave her a wave. She handed a tablecloth to a woman on the porch then disappeared back into the *haus*. Mary quickened her pace, caught up with Anna in her kitchen and smothered her in a hug. "Slow down, Anna, and don't work so hard. We are all here to help you."

Anna stepped back and drew a deep breath. "*Danki* for bringing all the rolls and bread, but there is a lot to do. Would you mind taking this tub out to the table for the dirty dishes?"

"Of course." Mary set it at one end of the table where they had the plates, glasses and beverages. She wandered toward the other end where the women were gathering and noticed that something had their attention.

Mary weaved around a few women and gasped. Noah! He had brought breakfast and lunch sandwiches from his store, along with delicious-looking coffee cake, rolls, fresh salads and jugs of beverages with his logo. And he was handing out plates of deli food and telling everyone to visit his store. He had his nerve. Heat rose up Mary's neck and burned on her cheeks.

Mamm set a pie on the table, wrapped her arm around Mary and drew her close. "Your pastries look *wunderbaar.*"

Daed approached wearing a supportive smile. "Your red face is noticeable." His gaze bounced from Noah back to her. "This is the first time that many of the Plain folks have probably tried his food. They only want to try something new. Your baking is *gut.* Quit worrying, *honig.*"

She glanced skyward, counted to three.

"He's going to steal all of Sweet Delights' business."

"*Nein*, sweetie." *Mamm* shook her head. "You'll win the baking contest then your bakery will be filled with customers."

Mary swallowed her next words. *Lord, forgive me for my jealousy.*

Daed patted her arm. "I've got to get back to work." He grabbed a breakfast biscuit and a fruit jar filled with water and headed toward the barn.

As the morning slowly crawled on, Mary's baked goods disappeared. *Jah*, the Lord answered her prayer and gave her a *gut* lesson. She would have to learn to get along with Noah. Kalona was a small town, and her family's bakery would have to survive on a smaller income, or she'd have to figure out how to expand, that was for sure and for certain.

After lunch, while she cleaned the table, she noticed Anna and Thomas Miller and their family walking around thanking the workers. They stopped next to her and Thomas cleared a tear-choked throat. "*Danki* for bringing all the *wunderbaar* food, Mary. We appreciate all the time you and Amanda donated to making it all."

"We were glad to do it." Mary glanced at the other end of the table. "Have you all met Noah Miller?" They shook their heads, but no one had a surprised look on their face. "I'll introduce you."

Noah looked up from unpacking a box as she led the small parade to his side. He gave a nod in greeting.

Mary gestured. "This is Noah Miller. Noah—" she motioned as she introduced each one "—these are your *grosseldre*, Thomas and Anna Miller, your *Onkel* Cyrus and his *frau*, Lois, and their son John, and your *Aent* Judith."

She stepped back while Noah told his family about his business and his sisters. But Mary could see the uneasiness in Thomas and Cyrus as they fidgeted with their straw hats and suspenders and looked around at the crowd that was still milling around the tables glancing over at them. Their Plain community was no doubt wondering if they were going to accept their long-lost son's family. This was big news! But she could tell by their stiff posture and stoic faces, it would be a slow process for Thomas and his family to accept Noah, if they ever did.

Cyrus abruptly nodded. "*Danki* for coming." His eyes darted to the men working on the barn, then back. "But we must get back to work." He turned and walked away, his frau following.

Thomas attempted a weak smile at Mary. "Your food was *gut. Danki* for coming." He turned to Noah. "Danki for all the gut breakfast sandwiches and food you brought." Thomas moseyed across the yard in the direction of the new barn.

Anna patted Noah's arm and smiled before heading toward the *haus*.

Mary watched Noah's brow furrow and a sad puppy dog expression cover his eyes. Her heart sank to the bottom of her feet. His whole family as much as rejected him, and earlier she begrudged him the right to bring his food and hand it out.

Aent Judith stepped closer to Noah as her family dispersed. "They'll come around, give them time. You look like your *daed*." She smiled. "Jeremiah was handsome, too."

Noah shrugged with a heightened color in his cheeks. "I knew when I drove out here to granddad's farm that my parents had left the community during their *rumspringa,* got married and never went home again. There are bound to be hard feelings."

"Is that all your *vater* told you? They left during *rumspringa*?" Judith sounded surprised.

"Pretty much. Dad said they didn't want to follow the strict church rules and have the community run their lives."

"Really, that was what he said?" Judith huffed as if exasperated.

Noah nodded.

"Did your *daed* tell you that he was helping our *vater* shingle the roof of the barn? When they ran short of shingles, Jeremiah rode to town to get another bundle. While he was gone, *Daed* fell off the roof and lay on the ground for hours before anyone found him. Cyrus believes that *Daed* limps because he didn't get medical attention soon enough."

Noah gasped. "*Nein*, he never said anything like that."

"When my husband was alive," Judith continued, "we went to see Jeremiah. I asked him to come back to the community, but he refused. He said he didn't feel worthy to be Amish and live in community."

Mary gasped as the hidden pieces rolled out of Judith's mouth. Had Sarah known all this and hadn't told her? Embarrassment rose to her face as she glanced at Noah. He probably didn't appreciate her eavesdropping. His face had paled. She took a step back then another but noticed several sets of eyes and ears trained their way. There were others interested, too.

Noah's shoulders sagged as he heaved a

sigh. "I always wondered if something happened to cause them to leave."

Someone tapped Mary on the shoulder. She turned and drew in a sharp breath.

Seth.

She grabbed his arm and pulled him away from Noah and Judith. Her gaze drifted from Seth's blue chambray shirt to his broadcloth trousers held by suspenders.

"So you left the *Englisch* ways and have returned?" her voice strained as she fought for control. "How did the bishop let you back in our community when they shunned you? Has it been a year already?" She took a couple steps back from him.

"I went to Davenport and worked a few months in a small factory. But those *Englischers* did a lot of drinking after work so I didn't have any real friends. It wasn't quite what I expected. I had a small apartment in an old house, but I had to share a bathroom." He paused and kicked at a stick on the ground. "It was lonely. I wanted to go back home, but my bruder said *Daed* was still angry. I ran into a cousin. He said his daed needed help and asked me to come and live with them. They farm in a small Plain community by Des Moines. They knew I was shunned, but their bishop reduced my punishment time from twelve to nine months and took me in. I repented, and he performed the rite of restoration. It's been a year, so Bishop Yoder accepted me back into our community."

"So why did you come back here?" She held back the real question she wanted to ask. *Was it worth giving up our love?*

"I missed *Mamm* and *Daed* and my *bruders*. I'm back in the furniture business with my family. It's a fine living." He nodded toward Noah. "You introduced him to his family. Are you *gut* friends with him?"

"I know him. His store is right across the street from Sweet Delights." She could hear a defensive sound in her voice.

"He's *Englisch*, Mary. Stay away from him."

She snorted. "*Jah*, this advice comes from

the man who left me standing at the altar so he could run after the *Englisch* ways."

He shrugged. "He's *Englisch* and you don't want to leave your faith. I know, it's not worth it."

She stared at him. "I don't need you telling me what I should do. You gave up that right. Remember?"

Seth nodded. "You're right. I did, but Noah's *mamm* and my *daed* were *bruder* and *schwester*. So your friend and I are cousins, and I'm not going to let him hurt you."

Mary turned on her heel, stomped to the table, grabbed her bag, the box of pans and headed to her buggy. Seth had his nerve talking to her like that. She tossed the box on the seat, flopped down and shook the reins. Did he think he still had the right to tell her what to do? Maybe he thought they'd just pick up where they'd left off?

She urged King into a fast trot and braced herself when the buggy swayed with the increased speed. The horse no doubt felt her tension in the reins.

Gritting her teeth, Mary tossed her ex-fiancé out of her head as her thoughts fluttered back to Noah and the confusion on his face as he learned about his family. He looked hurt, and her heart went out to him.

After she turned onto the highway, a cool breeze blew across her face and pulled her attention to the fields of corn swaying and rustling as their green stalks poked and pushed each other. She relaxed against the seat. She could never leave her Amish faith like Seth had. It was clear, too, that he never said he missed her.

Back in town, she unhitched King, carried her clanking pans into Sweet Delights and set them on the sink.

Amanda hurried through the kitchen doorway. "*Gut*, you're back. We're busy. How was your day?"

"Not as *gut* as Noah Miller's day. His food was a success. Everyone loved it and gathered around his table. He brought fresh salads and sandwiches made with his homemade breads."

"*Jah*, but our customers still stop in here for what they like best from Sweet Delights, right?" Amanda reasoned.

"You're not helping me feel better. I'm going to practice my apple pie and forget about Noah Miller."

Amanda stammered, "That reminds me, the bishop stopped by while you were gone."

Mary's feet froze to the spot. "What did he say?"

Her friend kept her chin down as she loaded a tray with cupcakes and cookies. "He said he'd talk to you later." She hesitated. "But his demeanor seemed serious." She gave Mary a quick glance before she scooped up more cookies and placed them on the tray. "On the other hand," she chuckled, "he always has a serious demeanor."

Mary blotted her forehead with her sleeve then pulled a bag of apples from the refrigerator. "He'll stop back if he has something to tell me." She peeled a couple of apples. "Amanda, did you know that Seth is back in town?"

The kitchen went silent as Amanda stood still. "How did you find out Seth is back?"

"So you did know."

"I'm sorry. I wasn't sure if he would stay or not, and I didn't want you to be hurt more by gossip if he wasn't back for *gut*."

"It would have been nice to know instead of getting blindsided."

Amanda turned toward Mary. "Did you talk to him?"

"He came up to me and warned me about being friendly with the *Englischer* Noah Miller. Of all people, him, the one who left me at the altar for the *Englisch* life. Now he has left that life and come back."

"Are you still in *liebe* with Seth?"

"Nein." The truth was she and Seth had always been friends. But she could never trust him again with her heart. She could never trust an *Englischer* or any man ever again with her heart.

After his family returned to the barn raising, Noah helped clean tables then hurried and placed his empty pans in a carton and set them in his vehicle. He needed to get back to town. He'd seen the way Mary eyed his deli food when he handed it out, the same way she had at the fire station bake sale. He could see the hurt in her eyes, and he wanted to explain to her. She probably thought he was trying to steal her customers.

And after meeting his family and his conversation with *Aent* Judith, he felt empty, like the last swallow of coffee had been sipped from the cup. He headed to the kitchen to find grandma. He stepped inside the house, glanced around the room of women and found her at the sink. "Grandma, I'm leaving now."

She whirled around, charged toward him and laid her damp hands on his shoulders. "*Danki* for coming and be sure to come back. And bring your sisters." Tears glistened in her eyes and rolled down her cheeks. She gave his shoulders a shake, then released him.

He nodded. "Sure." He cleared the frog from his throat and hurried to his SUV.

The four miles back to town went slowly at first, with several horses and buggies in front of him on the gravel road making their way home. After turning onto the highway, he made better time. Noah parked behind the store, dropped off his pans in the kitchen and stuck his head in the office to tell Jenny he was back.

"Noah, before you leave, I want to introduce you to your new assistant manager, Jean Dwyer." Jenny gestured to a woman sitting with her in the office. "She'll start on Monday."

"It's nice to meet you," Noah said with a quick nod. "I just have to run across the street to Sweet Delights for a minute, then I'll be back. If you have time, I'd like to show you around?"

"Yes, thanks, that would be great," she responded. "That way I'll know the ropes when I come in on Monday."

Noah jogged across the street to Sweet

Delights, his pulse racing; he thumped the door open with sweaty palms, giving the bell a hard shaking.

Mary startled from filling the coffee maker, turned, and met his gaze. "Hallo, Noah."

"Mary, I wanted to explain about taking all the food out to my grandpa's farm."

She waved a hand. "You don't owe me an explanation. They are your *grosseldre* and you had every right to do so. I'm sure they appreciated it."

"You're not just saying that?"

A grin plucked at the corners of her mouth before it stretched into a full grin. "As you *Englisch* say, you knocked it out of the park."

At first, her words startled Noah, and he wasn't sure how to take it. He blew out a long breath. "Thanks for understanding." He nodded. "See you later." As the door closed behind him, his heart rate began to slow to normal.

As he crossed the street and thought about his grandparents, a weird notion pulled

Noah in two different directions: one toward his Amish family and one toward the *Englisch* world.

He'd grown up in the *Englisch* world whether firmly planted in it or not, but that's where he was comfortable. Yet his family was Amish.

So which one was he? Amish or *Englisch*?

Chapter Six

Mary gazed out the bakery window into a fiery-red sun rising over the horizon. The breeze pushed the clouds into a race across the sky and set her feet in motion to get to work. She grabbed a set of tongs and helped Amanda unload the pastry cart into the display case. "I can't believe we're running so late this morning."

Amanda cackled. "That's what we get for sipping coffee and eating our own rolls."

Mary watched two women stroll by the window carrying cups and bags from Noah's store, followed by three men who were usually her morning customers. She stomped back to the kitchen and grabbed a stack of empty pans off the cart, banging them as she set them on the sink.

Amanda jumped at the noise. "Is something wrong?"

"If I leave early today, can you close the bakery?"

"Of course. What's going on?"

"I'm tired of seeing Noah's deli cups go by the windows. I'm going to order a cappuccino and latte machine. Sweet Delights has to serve those fancy coffee beverages that women *liebe*. We are losing too much business."

She had to hand it to Noah, though. He knew what the public liked. Nein, it wasn't jealousy. It was a matter of learning how to compete with an *Englisch* store right across the street. But she'd learn.

After the rush of Thursday's lunch crowd, Mary retreated to the office and pulled out brochures of cappuccino and latte makers. She read each one and noticed the different features that each offered. Since she'd only had one cappuccino, it was hard to pick.

At 2:00 p.m., Mary hitched King to the buggy, but first there was one stop to make before the supply store.

She needed $1,000 to pay for the cappuccino and latte maker. It was expensive, but surely her *stiefmutter* would see the need. If Sarah didn't have the money, Mary could sell something, but what? The only thing she had of value was the quilt in her cedar chest that her *mamm* had made her before she died of cancer.

Tears clouded her eyes. Mary grabbed a handkerchief from her bag, blotted her tears and blew her nose. *Nein*, she couldn't sell the quilt *Mamm* had hand stitched it, each day growing paler as the quilt grew lovelier. She had very few things left that *Mamm* had made.

The quilt would easily bring $800.

Nein, Mary would ask Sarah for the money. She'd understand.

When they reached the farm, King slowed,

turned into the driveway without coaxing and headed for the barn. *Jah*, this horse never missed a feeding. She didn't unhitch him but hung a bucket of oats on the barn door and hurried to the *haus*.

When she entered the kitchen, Sarah stood at the table making pastry.

"You're home early dear."

Mary slung her bag on a chair. "*Mamm*, we have to buy an espresso machine for the bakery. We can't compete with Noah's store unless we expand the menu, and those fancy drinks are favorites of everyone."

Sarah gave the dough two more passes with the rolling pin and placed the piecrust in a pan. She scrubbed her hands together over the wastebasket to remove the flour and bits of dough, then rinsed them under the faucet and dried.

Mary watched her *stiefmutter* and knew she was taking her time thinking about the answer.

"Mary, a *gut* commercial espresso machine would cost more than a thousand dollars. I'm sorry, but we just don't have that kind of money. Your *daed* wants to get the twins' hospital bill paid before we buy anything else."

A child's scream rose from the corner of the kitchen and drew Mary's attention to the chaos. Michael Paul had his wooden barn set up and the twins, Lena and Liza, were doing their best to aggravate him by hitting his animals.

"*Mamm*," Michael Paul pouted, "tell the twins to quit knocking my cows over."

"In a minute, Michael, I will put them down for a nap."

"*Mamm,*" Mary pressed, "if we don't expand the menu, the bakery will be driven out of business."

Sarah stepped beside Mary and patted her shoulder. "You need to work on the recipe that'll win the contest next month. Are you even sure Sweet Delights needs an expanded menu?"

Mary scowled. "What do you mean?"

"Our bakery has faithful, local customers

and we have a lot of tourist business. Yes, revenue may drop, has dropped, but maybe we need to create new recipes and try that first. Many of Iowa City's bakeries have fancy cupcakes in the windows, pies with lattice work or braiding around the edges and flavored drizzles over the tops."

Mary placed a hand on the back of a chair to steady herself. "So you think that my baking is causing us to lose customers?"

"*Nein*, I didn't say that. I noticed a cooking magazine in the doctor's office the other day, and I've been meaning to talk to you about it. I also went into Noah's store yesterday."

"You did what?" Mary gasped.

"Sweetheart, if we want to compete, our product has to be better." Sarah walked to the counter and took the metal lid off a cake plate. There sat a dozen mini cupcakes with paper holders stamped with Noah's store logo. Each cupcake was a different flavor and piled high with swirled frosting and some with syrupy drizzle.

"Did you and *Daed* try Noah's cupcakes?" Mary's voice cracked, disbelief choking her words.

"Mary, his baking is delicious. Now he has started to make Amish spoonbread, friendship bread, and whoopee pies in all kinds of flavors. He uses glazes and flavored drizzles over cakes and cookies. They are attractive desserts."

Pulling a chair away from the kitchen table, Mary plopped down. "*Mamm*, we are Amish. We have never made our desserts look fancy. What will the bishop think?"

"It's only different colored frosting. What can he say?" Sarah sat across from Mary. "While I was looking at Noah's pastries and candy, I overheard two women talking. They said his hazelnut toffee and truffles won a contest in Iowa City."

Sarah's words dug sharply under Mary's skin. "I—I didn't know he was that *gut*." Her stomach did a flip. "I thought, or maybe I was hoping, it was his cheap prices that were bringing in the customers."

Sarah raised a brow. "He has sandwich cookies with faces made out of chocolate chips and candy acorn noses. Some *kinner* were squealing and saying how much they loved them." She grabbed a cookie from the jar and some chocolate chips, sat back at the table and showed Mary a simple design. "The customers don't want a plain sugar cookie or a plain gingerbread man."

"*Mamm*, the way you're talking, we need to rethink our whole baking strategy, too."

"We'll work on the decorations. We'll get together with Hannah, my former assistant. She is very clever and a *wunderbaar* baker." Sarah patted Mary's arm, then went back to her pie and dumped the bowl of cherries she had pitted into the shell.

After pouring a cup of coffee, Mary sipped the hot brew, thoughts spinning in all directions. Hard to believe Noah had that kind of talent. Funny, she hadn't noticed that on her one whirlwind tour through his store on opening day. He clearly kept changing his sale items to keep his customers interested, inquisitive and coming back. *So, Mr. Englischer, you think you can outsmart and outbake us...me.*

Mary's heart fluttered when an image of the handsome Noah Miller breezed through her mind. He was sure a cute cookie, but she was going to crumble that big ego of his.

She pushed her chair back, grabbed her bag and headed for the stairs. Mary closed her bedroom door and opened her cedar chest. She picked up the double-wedding-ring quilt that her real *mamm* had made. Caressing a hand across the quilting and over her favorite pastel colors, she hugged it to her chest. Tears blurred her vision.

Rolling the folded quilt tightly, she tied it with a ribbon and stuffed it in her bag. Mary hurried downstairs and out the kitchen door while Sarah's back was turned. She jumped in the buggy and headed to the consignment shop in Kalona.

Early Monday morning, Noah walked into the office and watched Jenny stare intently at the computer screen. "Hope there's not a problem."

She glanced his way before returning her gaze to the monitor. "No, just trying to catch up. I'm going to start interviewing applicants in a little while for my replacement, but Emily needs to get registered for school today. She's at Sweet Delights. Would you mind taking her to sign up? It'll be a good test for your new assistant Jean to see how she manages without your watchful eye."

Noah quirked an eyebrow at his sister, "I've trained her well, she'll do fine."

He ran across the street and opened the bakery door to the mingling aromas of cinnamon coffee and caramel topping of some kind. His eyes roamed aver the full tables and chairs to Emily sitting at a table with an older couple.

As he walked to the counter, his gaze swept across the new espresso machine. He stopped short when he saw the display case and the expanded assortment of sweets, whoopee pies, red velvet cookies and fruit-filled cookie snaps. He could barely resist trying one.

Mary looked up as he approached. "Mornin', Noah."

"Good morning, Mary. I see you decided to add cappuccino and lattes to your menu."

She smiled. "Afraid of the competition?"

"No, not from you." He held eye contract for a second before she looked away. If she would have stared at him a second longer with those blue eyes, he would have bought all her cookies. Feud or not, she was sure cute.

The doorbell jingled and Mary glanced at the customer. Her shoulders squared and the smile vanished from her face. Noah turned to see who had created such a reaction in her. A twinge of jealousy stung his heart. Seth.

His cousin entered the shop and stopped. He shot Mary a warm smile then yanked his gaze over to Noah. "*Hallo*, cousin."

Noah nodded at Seth. He had wanted to meet his family. But it had been a shock to find out that Seth, his mother's nephew, was the man who had broken Mary's heart.

Seth took a step toward Noah and held out his hand. Noah grabbed a hold and shook, but Seth didn't let go.

Noah jerked his hand away and stepped back.

"Since the dust of shame has settled after your parents' desertion, you've come sneaking back to claim your inheritance, right?"

"Sneaking?" Noah straightened his back. "I opened a store. That's not really sneaking."

"Your *daed* was the youngest son and the one to inherit the Miller farm. So now you're back to step into that role. Your *Onkel* Cyrus and his son, John Miller, aren't happy to see you snooping around their farm."

"Like I said, I own a store here in Kalona, and I own another in Iowa City. I didn't come here to work on a farm or to steal one from anyone." Noah glanced at Emily still sitting with the elderly couple at the table. He motioned for her to head to the door.

Emily hurried out in front of Noah. "Was he the man you were looking for?" she asked.

"What?" He strode across the street. "Well, not the one I had in mind, but he is a cousin of ours. He is the son of Mom's brother."

"He acted sort of angry." Emily glanced back toward the bakery.

Noah grunted. "He's jealous of Mary. He likes her and doesn't like that I talk to her. Do you understand jealousy?"

"Yes. Mom gave me a lecture once when I was jealous of a girl because she had a pretty dress on and mine was a plain one that Mom had made. I wanted one like the other girl wore. Mom said it's what God sees on your inside that makes Him smile, not what's on the outside. You have a good inside, Noah."

Noah reached over and squeezed Emily's hand. As young as she was, she could apply the lesson to this situation. It was the will of God that they should try to please, and then all else would fall into place. But how did anyone decipher the will of God? Noah was still trying to figure that out.

Chapter Seven

Mary slung her hands on her hips, traipsed around the counter and lowered her voice. "Please leave, Seth. I don't appreciate you coming into my bakery and making a scene in front of my customers."

Seth puffed his chest. "He needs to know how things are. He can't expect to move into our community and weasel his way into our *gut* graces."

Mary shook her head. "Farming is the last thing on Noah's mind, and who gets the Miller farm is none of your business, even if you are friends with John Miller." She nodded toward the door. "*Good*bye, Seth." He turned on his heels and marched out.

She returned to the counter, feeling her customer's eyes boring into her back. Business was bad enough without Seth coming in and making a scene.

She grabbed a cloth, cleaned the counter and tidied up around the coffeepots. When the bakery was empty, she hustled to the kitchen, trying to shake off his outburst. She pulled a bowl from the cupboard, scooped up a bag of apples, and peeled.

"Going to practice your apple pie again?" Amanda pulled two loaves of cinnamon bread from the oven and set them on a cooling rack.

She tossed a peeling in the sink. "There is something about the crust that just isn't right. It's dense instead of flaky, and the apple filling is tart. It will never win a contest."

"Add more butter." Amanda pulled a package from the refrigerator and handed it to Mary.

"Danki." She dumped three cups of flour in the bowl, added the baking powder, salt and sugar. She worked in the butter, poured in the milk and added the spiced apples.

Mary glanced at the recipe for caramel sauce. She added sugar to an iron skillet and stirred continuously until it turned into light brown syrup. Gradually, she added the boiling water and let it simmer.

The trick to a delicious tasting sauce was getting the sugar to the perfect color before adding the water. Sarah had shown her how to create depth of taste. But it wasn't easy and sometimes it took her more than one try. On contest day, she'd have to make it perfect the first time. This recipe was spectacular...when it turned out right.

Mary washed her hands and took her floured apron off. "Amanda, can you watch the bakery for a little while? I have an order to pick up at Hochstetler's Cheese and Ice Cream shop."

"Of course. Tell, Fredda *hallo.* Ice cream will help you forget your fussing with Seth."

"You saw his little outburst?"

"*Nein.* I heard it all the way in the kitchen, along with everyone else in the bakery."

Mary gritted her teeth. "Seth better never set foot in this bakery again. People will be talking, especially since the gossip has just calmed down after he dumped me at the altar. We have enough trouble keeping customers without him acting like a hooligan."

Amanda's eyes widened, and she shook her head. "Seth did that because he still cares for you. He knows what he lost, and he doesn't want you mixed up with another sweet-talking, *gut*-looking *Englischer.*"

"Amanda, you are a hopeless romantic." Mary collected her bag from the closet and opened the door to a thick, humid breath of August air. The blazing Midwest heat pressed in on her, propelling her quickly down the two blocks to Hochstetler's Cheese and Ice Cream.

Mary entered the shop, weaved around the cheese-tasting tables, the coolers and headed to the counter.

When Fredda saw her, she ran around the counter and crushed her in a hug. "I'm so glad to see you, Mary. We have your order all ready. Come and look at our new cheeses, and I'll pour two glasses of tea."

Mary browsed the cooler. There was goat cheese, cheddar, Swiss, Colby, shredded, sliced...and dozens more. Mary took a sample of Swiss on a cracker and turned toward Fredda as she approached. "This is delicious."

"Danki. How did your customers like the ice cream? Would you like to try some different flavors?" Fredda held up a tiny sugar cone.

Mary laughed. "*Danki*, but *nein*. They love the last order, but I'd never get out of here if I started sampling. You have really expanded since the last time I was here. You've done a *wunderbaar* job fixing this shop to display your cheeses."

"*Danki*, would you like to try some different cheeses?" Fredda turned the plate of samples around and pushed it closer to Mary.

"Not right now. I'm going to expand the

bakery's menu and start having biscuits and croissants for breakfast and sandwiches for lunch. When we've updated the bakery, I'll start out with the ones I ordered for today, then maybe add Swiss and provolone."

"*Jah*, whatever you want. I can give you some samples to try."

Mary finished her tea and caught up on all Fredda's news. "Danki, but I need to get back to the bakery." She bumped the door open with her hip, maneuvered her bags through the opening, and stepped down to the sidewalk and smack-dab into the path of a man.

Her bag of cheese dropped to the sidewalk. She wobbled back and forth then lost her balance. The man reached around her and pulled her up to a standing position. Cars passing by honked, and a buggy slowed down to nearly a crawl. *Ach.* She glanced at the street, people were watching.

"*Danki*, but please take your hands off me." Heat burned from her cheeks to the top of her ears.

"I'm so sorry. I didn't see you." His voice sounded all too familiar.

She jerked her head up to see his face.

"Noah Miller. I might have known it would be you." She started to reach down.

"I'll get the bag." He picked it up. "Sorry, I was looking across the street and didn't notice you coming out of the shop. It's my fault. I'll carry your bags back to the bakery."

"Please don't. I can manage." Mary glanced around and noticed cars still slowing to watch them, trying to figure out what had happened.

"I insist after nearly knocking you out."

"Noah, I don't want you anywhere near me. You and Seth made a public display in my shop. Some of those customers will probably never come back. You humiliated me, then and now."

Mary brushed her hands down her dress to smooth her skirt and noticed red smudges. She glanced at her palms, scraped, bleeding and covered with dirt. She snatched the bags from his hands. "You are bound to destroy me one way or another."

Her gaze landed on his face and caught the grin he tried to conceal with his hand.

"So this is funny to you?" She tried to make her voice sound serious when she was stifling a laugh.

He pushed the smile away and gulped. "No, of course not, but what a coincidence."

"You are impossible." She turned, the bags crinkling in her hands, and hurried down the sidewalk.

Amanda was right. Noah was certainly handsome, but he was dangerous territory. He had an invisible off-limits sign posted to his forehead. Mary had made a mistake trusting Seth. She wouldn't make that same error again with another *Englischer*...and certainly not this one.

Tuesday morning, Noah climbed into his SUV and headed for his grandparents' farm. He turned onto the gravel road and just before their driveway, he saw his grandpa standing along the side of the road, pliers in hand, mending fence.

Noah pulled onto the shoulder and parked. He blotted moist hands on his trousers and forced himself out of the vehicle. With each step over the road bank, dry grass and weeds snapped and rustled under his feet, but his grandpa stayed focused on his work. Thomas Miller's abrupt manner had made it clear at their last meeting that he didn't care to mingle with *Englisch* folks. And that was what Noah was. *Englisch.*

Noah stepped to the side of his grandpa and cleared his throat, but the old man didn't acknowledge his presence. "It's a hot day to mend fence."

Grandpa grasped the pliers around the wire fencing with one hand, pulled it up tight to the wooden post, grabbed a staple from his pouch and nailed it in place with the other hand. The old man had a system, but it looked awkward to do with only one set of hands.

When he finished with that post, he silently walked around Noah and headed down the fence line watching for weak spots. He came to another piece of wiring that had pulled loose. Before his grandfather could grab his hammer from his tool belt, Noah pulled it out, snatched a staple from his pouch, placed it over the wire, and hammered it into the post.

In silence, they walked down to the next spot that needed fixing. Grandpa pulled the sagging fence up tight against the post. Noah stuck his hand in the staple pouch, pricked his finger on a sharp edge but pulled a staple out and hammered it into the post. When he finished, a drop of blood had smeared onto the staple and post.

"Your hands will be riddled with blisters and cuts if you keep on working without gloves." The old man pulled a pair of gloves from his waistband and handed them to Noah.

He slid them on as they walked farther down the fence. In silence, they mended post after post. Not what Noah had expected, but he enjoyed helping his grandfather.

They worked another two hours. At noon, grandpa glanced up at the sun, turned and headed back toward his driveway.

Noah followed. When he came to the spot where he'd parked, he headed for his vehicle.

"Anna will have lunch ready, and I always feed my help before I send them home," Grandpa said as he kept on walking.

Stunned at the invitation, the words hit Noah like a steel bat. To reject would no doubt insult him, and he knew this situation was as hard on his grandparents as it was on him.

Noah pivoted and followed his grandpa to the house. When the old man hung his straw hat on a peg by the door, Noah hung his hat on the peg next to it.

"Anna, set another place." Grandpa motioned to the sink. "Wash up in the metal basin."

Grandma handed Noah a towel. He wiped

his hands and handed it to his grandpa then sat at the new place setting. When his grandparents sat, he bowed his head for silent prayer and took his food when they passed the bowls and platter.

The silence was unnerving. But unfamiliar with Amish customs, Noah didn't want to talk if they weren't allowed to speak at the dinner table.

"Why are you here?" His grandpa's gruff voice shook the silence.

"I stopped by to...just say hello."

"*Nein,* I mean why did you move to Kalona if you have a store in Iowa City?" Grandpa kept his head down and continued to eat.

"I wanted to expand the business. The store in Iowa City is doing well, but Kalona is a huge tourist attraction because of the Amish community."

"So you thought you'd tell them you were Amish and get more business?"

Noah dropped his fork. It clanked against the plate then settled in his smashed potatoes. "No, nein. that's not what I'm doing.

I'm just opening a store like anyone else. I've told a few people that my parents were Amish, but I don't advertise it." His back stiffened, and his appetite waned. He pushed his chair away from the table.

Grandpa motioned toward Noah's plate. "Finish eating."

Noah hesitated, but pulled his chair back to the table and took a bite of food. Maybe this wasn't a good idea. But if he didn't try, how was he ever going to get to know them?

Tension hung in the air like the dust from the gravel road, and silence clung to the steam rising from the food.

Noah finished eating. "You're a good cook, Grandma. Thank you for inviting me to dinner. It was a pleasure getting a chance to help you and share a meal with you two." The words pushed out on their own, surprising even Noah.

He shoved his chair back, gave a nod to his grandpa and retrieved his hat from the peg. "Goodbye."

He headed back to his SUV. His stomach

was full, but his heart felt half-empty. He wasn't sure why he wanted a relationship with his grandparents, but he did. He missed his parents, and he missed not knowing his family.

He opened his vehicle door and looked back at his grandparents' house. He understood their reserved feelings, especially about the *Englisch*. His parents had said the Amish lived apart because they separated themselves from the fallen world. From nonbelievers.

He was a believer. Was it possible for him to have a relationship with them? And to have one with Mary?

Chapter Eight

After completing the Wednesday morning baking, Mary flipped open her recipe book. Was she wasting her time looking for that special recipe? The bishop hadn't given her his final approval to enter the contest yet, and it was in five weeks.

She pulled a pencil from a holder and added notes to her recipe card: more nutmeg and a dash of cinnamon. Maybe she'd add licorice or anise for a little different taste to the apples and try a cookie dough for the pie crust.

Mary mixed, rolled the dough, laid the butter crust in the pan, arranged the spiced apples, and then wove strips of pastry over the top. She slipped it in the oven just as the bell jingled over the front door. Blotting her hands on her apron, she speed-walked toward the display counter. When she saw the customer, her feet almost stuttered to a stop. Bishop Yoder. And he wore a solemn face.

She eased herself forward like a child en route to her father for punishment. Reaching the counter, she jerked her chin up. "*Gut Morgen*, Bishop Yoder. Do you have a sweet tooth this morning?"

"Just a cup of coffee, and could you take a minute to sit with me?"

"*Jah*, I'll bring it over." Her hands jittered as she poured the coffee.

He took the table by the window and placed his hat on the chair next to him.

Oh, Lord, please let this be gut *news.* She carried two cups to the table and sat opposite the bishop. She blew on her coffee while he poured sugar and cream into his brew and stirred.

He took a sip, pushed his cup to the side

and clasped his hands on the table. "Mary, I was riding past Hochstetlers' Cheese shop on Monday, and I noticed you with Noah Miller. He had his arms around you. I'm sure I don't need to remind you of the problems with seeing an *Englischer.* You're a baptized member of the church. You will be shunned if you marry him, and the church could discipline you if continue to make such a public display."

Mary jerked her cup as she raised it to take a sip. Nearly spilling it, she set it back down. "I'm not seeing Noah."

"I know that he and his sisters spend significant time at your bakery."

"Emily likes to come over and talk to Amanda, and she enjoys helping us bake. She's new in town and lonely. It's harmless." Her words flurried out, uncontrolled.

"I also saw you with Noah at the barn raising introducing him to his relatives. Be careful, Mary." He emphasized the last three words. "What looks like something innocent today can turn into something serious when you least suspect it." The bishop took another sip of his coffee, grabbed his hat and pushed his chair back. "You have permission to compete in the contest." He stood and walked out.

At the sound of footfalls behind her, Mary sprang up from her chair. "Amanda, you gave me a start. I didn't hear you come in."

"*Jah*, I see that. You're as white as flour. Are you all right?"

"The bishop was just here and warned me about getting too friendly with Noah. But I got permission to compete in the contest."

"*Gut* news and bad. He's trying to keep his flock together. You can't blame him for that. And he knows that kind of relationship can end in heartbreak." Amanda wrapped her friend in a hug. "But you don't have feelings for Noah, do you?" Her voice sounded more probing than sure.

"Of course not." At least, Mary hoped she didn't. Although her back still tingled from Noah's touch after he lifted her from the ground. Her heart fluttered each time she thought about the encounter. But *nein*, she would be sure to protect her heart when Noah was around. She followed Amanda back to the kitchen.

"*Ach*, my pie smells done." Mary grabbed potholders and pulled the hot tin from the oven. A loud thump at the front door startled her. Her hands jerked, but she managed to get the pie to the counter before it slipped to the floor. "What is that commotion?"

"I have no idea." Amanda dropped her rolling pin and raced ahead of Mary to the front of the bakery.

Daed and Jacob carried a table into the bakery and set it by the window. Mary laughed and blew out a sigh. "Sorry, Amanda, I forgot to tell you that we are going to start serving breakfast biscuits and croissants in the mornings."

"What?" Amanda stared at the two new tables and chairs they were carrying inside and squeezing in next to the other five. "Mary, that's going to be a lot of work for just the two of us."

"The business has to expand in order to compete with Noah's store. We are just going to offer the biscuit and croissant from six to nine a.m. It shouldn't take much more effort to fry a few eggs, bacon and ham. My cousin Nettie is going to come in and help us.

Daed wrapped his arm around Mary. "I pray your business will improve. Now, Jacob and I must get back to the farm."

Mary ran her hand across one of the wooden tables *Daed* had made. He loved to work with his hands, and it showed. She picked up a piece of chalk and wrote on the chalkboard. Starting Friday, breakfast biscuits and croissants being served with egg, ham or bacon.

On Thursday, Mary and Amanda arrived early to make sure the kitchen was organized and there was space ready for additional biscuits and croissants. Later in the morning, the Country Fresh truck delivered the extra eggs, ham and bacon.

"I sure hope my idea works." Mary braced herself with a hand on the edge of the counter. Her brain spinning at the thought of the extra money she had spent.

"It will." Amanda patted her friend on the back. "You'll see."

Mary drew a deep, cleansing breath. "Well, at least Noah's store isn't in the Kalona tourist guide yet, so the tourists will probably stop at Sweet Delights first. But I'm sure he'll have it listed for next year's printing."

She put that out of her head as she started her long day of baking and preparing the bakery for serving a hot breakfast.

After Amanda set the croissant dough in the refrigerator and went home, Mary took one last survey of the kitchen's layout, turned the lights out, locked up and hurried, feet aching, to the buggy. She hitched King, and as she stepped in the buggy, a thought tickled her brain. Tomorrow, Noah would be in for a surprise when Sweet Delights started selling fresh breakfast biscuits and croissants.

* * *

Friday morning Mary's cousin, Nettie Brenneman, met her at the bakery and followed her in to the kitchen. "Danki, Nettie, for helping us out.

"I'm glad to do it. What do you want me to do?"

"Why don't you get the skillets ready for bacon, ham and eggs? Place your supplies where it's comfortable for you. I'll take the croissant dough from the refrigerator and finish making the first batch."

"*Danki*, Mary, I'm excited about helping, and maybe I can show you some of my baking."

She watched Nettie tear around the kitchen, accustomed to cooking for her parents and ten siblings. Mary had tasted Nettie's breakfast rolls, and they were delicious. *Jah*, maybe Nettie would bring some new flavor to the bakery.

Ten minutes later, Amanda rushed into the kitchen, letting in a cool gust of morning air. She glanced around. "Wow, you two have been working hard. The stations look ready to go."

Mary glanced at her friend. "*Gut Morgen. Jah*, Nettie will fry the eggs and meat. I'm finishing the croissants."

"I'll start the biscuits." Amanda poured a cup of coffee, took a sip and got started.

Mary rolled out the croissant dough, shaped the triangles and brushed with egg wash. She set them aside to proof. When they were puffed up and spongy to the touch, she spritzed a preheated oven, placed the croissants in the oven and spritzed again. At the end of the process, they were a golden brown.

Fifteen minutes later, Mary glanced at the clock. "Almost time to start." She darted to the front of the bakery, set out condiments, and filled the napkins holders.

At 6:00 a.m., she unlocked the door. Before she had time to walk back to the counter, Frank Wallin pushed the door open.

He stuck his nose in the air and made a loud sniffing sound. "It smells like bacon in here. I'll try a ham, egg and cheese biscuit, and my usual roll and coffee."

"Frank," Mary chuckled, "did you order a roll because you're not sure if you'll like the biscuit?" A smile pulled at her mouth, but she tried to push it away.

He laughed. "It was a hard decision. I want to try the biscuit, but it's hard giving up the roll."

Amanda scooted in from the kitchen with the biscuit. "You're feeling daring today, Frank."

Mary bagged the biscuit and handed it to Frank along with his coffee. "Let us know how you like it?"

"I will, but I have no doubt that it's delicious."

After Frank, Mary served one customer after another. When the steady stream let up, she glanced at the clock. 9:00. "*Ach.* It was a success."

Amanda ran to the front. "Wunderbaar."

Nettie stuck her head around the kitchen door. "Congratulations!"

Mary laughed and twirled around. "I can't believe the difference that a few eggs and ham can make."

The doorbell jingling, pulled her attention to the next customer. She straightened and threw on a smile. Noah Miller.

Noah stepped forward. "So, you're making breakfast sandwiches now. You're sort of a copycat," he clowned.

"The bakery has to compete with other businesses, Noah, or was it your plan just to run me out of town without a fight?" Her cheeks reddened.

He laughed. "Take it easy. I'm just teasing you. I don't blame you one bit for serving breakfast. I'd do the same thing. I stopped to thank you for introducing me to my family out at the barn raising."

Her cheeks lightened to a pink. "Glad it worked out for you." Her tone was warm.

"I'm not sure how it *worked out* just yet, but at least we know each other now. I stopped by my grandpa's farm the other day. He was mending fence, I helped him, and he asked me to stay to dinner."

"That's *wunderbaar*. He is strict in his belief, but maybe he will soften."

"I don't know about that. I helped him, and I think he felt obligated."

"You should see it for what it is. The feet walk the road, but *Gott* works in the heart to change the direction."

"Maybe someday I'll know God well enough that I'll understand what you just said."

Mary poured a cup of coffee and handed it to Noah. "I think your *grossdaddi* wants to get to know you, but you are *Englisch*. Your *daed*, his *sohn*, broke his heart when he left and never came home to visit or try to patch up whatever happened between them. That had to be hard on Thomas."

"You're right. I'm expecting too much." Noah braced a hip against the counter.

Mary's eyes locked with his then she pulled away. "Just keep seeing him. Maybe you can melt the ice that has formed around his heart. Eventually, you may chip it away. Where's Emily? I haven't seen her the last few days."

"She started school and has met some friends, so you may not see her quite as much now." He tried to hide the smile that wanted to break free. Mary had actually dropped her guard and let them have a gentle moment.

"*Gut*, she needs friends."

He glanced at the display case. "So how is your recipe for the contest coming along?"

"So that's your real reason for stopping by. Now I understand. For your information, Mr. Miller, it is out-of-this-world wow-wee."

Noah laughed. "I have no doubt. You're a terrific baker. I haven't decided what I'm going to make yet. But I'm sure I'll find the perfect one that'll stand up to yours."

"Noah," she huffed, "you are so conceited."

"I can see I have overstayed my welcome. See you around, Chef Brenneman." He stole another quick look at Mary before heading to the door. She was sure feisty.

But then why shouldn't she be? She was fighting for her bakery and the welfare of her family. He understood, but he'd invested a lot of money in opening this store, and he couldn't afford to throw it away. The contest would help decide which one of them would survive.

Either way, he would lose. If he won the contest, it would probably drive her out of business, since a town with a population of five thousand probably couldn't sustain two bakeries year round. If she won, he'd be driven out of town.

He crossed the street and looked back at Sweet Delights. Either way, he would lose a friend, one that sure could irritate him but also kept him on his toes.

Chapter Nine

Mary sorted through Saturday's mail and opened the box of new tourist brochures that had just arrived and glanced through the top one. She browsed the column under restaurants and bakeries. Lazy Susan's headed the list, followed by Miller's Farm-fresh Grocery, Delicatessen and Bakery, then Sweet Delights.

She stared at the paper until the words began to blur. She threw the brochure back in the box and snapped the lid closed.

Amanda looked up from filling the display case. "Something wrong?"

"Noah's shop is listed."

"Oh! Well, at least yours is listed first, *jah*?"

"*Nein*, they didn't just add it at the end, they put the shops in alphabetical order. His is listed before Sweet Delights because they forgot the Amish in front."

She lifted the box cover, picked up a brochure and handed it to Amanda. Her friend glanced over it, groaned and handed it back. Mary set the box in the cupboard, pulled the remaining old brochures out and set a stack on the edge of the counter.

"So you are going to use up the old ones first?"

"Please don't judge me." Uneasiness stalked up Mary's back.

"I'm not judging you. I know your situation. That feeling you have is coming from you judging yourself. You paid for the old brochures and have a right to use them."

The doorbell jingled, and old Bishop Ropp entered, tapping a cane along the tile flooring. *"Gut Morgen."*

Mary hurried around the counter to his

side. "Bishop, can I help you? What happened?"

"I can manage. A cup of coffee and a piece of apple pie, please. And how about a sample of your contest entry dessert? I'll sit, rest and enjoy the pie…if someone gets it for me."

"*Jah, jah.* I'll hurry, but what happened? Are you feeling all right?"

"Old age is what happened. I think I can do anything I did when I was young, but my body lets my mind know who is really in charge. I twisted my knee trying to climb on my *sohn* Albert's hayrack. So like the old horses, I'm put out to pasture. If I keep coming in here for pie, I'll look like an old horse, too."

Mary hurried to the kitchen, returned and set two plates in front of the bishop. "Here is your pie. And this other one on your right—" she slid the plate closer "—is my contest entry. I'd like you to try it and tell me what you think?"

He took a bite of the pie in front of him,

chewed and glanced toward the ceiling. He took a bite of the second one. "Both *gut* but not as *wunderbaar* as Sarah's papa's pie. I thought you were going to try to find his recipe?"

"Sarah found his old recipe book, but it wasn't there, or he didn't write the recipe down that you're talking about. We'll probably never find it. But are you sure this isn't close?"

"*Jah*, I'm sure."

She sighed. "Looks like I'll be staying late again to practice."

Just before closing, Mary made a pie but the result was the same as before. She cleaned the kitchen, locked the back door, hitched King and set him to a brisk pace. When he turned into the driveway, Mary glanced across the barnyard and noticed Hannah Smith's, Sarah's former assistant, buggy parked in the drive by the house.

She'd better hurry and say hi to Hannah before she left. She unhitched and fed King, then dashed into the kitchen.

"*Ach*, Hannah, it's *gut* to see you."

"*Danki,*" Hannah pulled out the chair next to her at the table and pointed to it. "I was hoping I'd get to see you. Sarah was just telling me that you're going to enter the fall festival baking competition. How *wunderbaar.* That should give you a lot of publicity."

Mary sat next to Hannah. "I was hoping we could put our heads together and come up with a fantastic apple recipe. Bishop Ropp was in the bakery today and insists Sarah's *daed* had an apple pie recipe that he'd drive five miles just to eat a piece."

Hannah turned to Mary's *stiefmutter.* "What recipe is that, Sarah? Did we make it?"

"*Nein*, I don't think so. I did find an old recipe book in the attic that belonged to Daed. It had an apple pie recipe."

Mary nodded "I made it. Bishop Ropp tried a piece and said that wasn't it."

"While you two talk," Sarah stood, "I'll go back upstairs and look again."

Hannah shook her head at Sarah. "I've seen that mess up in the attic before. We'll all go. Remember, safety in numbers."

Sarah raised a brow. "It's not that bad."

Mary climbed up the narrow attic steps first and pushed the small door open. She ducked her head and entered, but the ceiling was so low she had to stay bent over. She held the lantern as her *stiefmutter* and Hannah entered. "I'll hold the light while you two search these boxes."

Sarah pointed to a cardboard box. "Check that one, Hannah. I'm going to dig through this big one."

Mary held the lantern high to shed light on both the boxes. Piece by piece, Sarah and Hannah picked through years of collecting.

"Here are some recipes," Sarah shouted. "They're loose ones in the very bottom of the box." She pulled them out and carefully shuffled through the yellow, brittle pages.

Mary inched the lantern closer so Sarah could get a *gut* look at the writing. "What are they, *Mamm*?"

Sarah held up one of the pages, a smile playing across her face. "This one is an apple pie recipe. All of these loose recipes must have fallen out of the book when I grabbed it the other day."

"You found it?" Mary stepped closer.

"Well, I found an apple pie recipe. You'll have to make it, let Bishop Ropp try it and see if it's the one."

"Let's get this stuff back in the boxes and get out of here." Hannah wiped her brow. "It's hot up here."

As Mary led the parade back into the kitchen, her *daed* entered from the porch. She held the recipe up for him to see. "We think we found the recipe that was lost."

"*Gut*. Have you told her yet, Sarah?"

"*Nein*, Caleb, I waited for you."

Mary glanced from Sarah to her *daed*. "What's going on?"

Her *daed* smiled. "Summer crops were *gut*. I have enough money to install additional kitchen electrical outlets and get it ready for the food-service expansion. That way, when you win the contest, you can install griddles, a panini press or whatever else you need. A carpenter will install a bar across the front of the bakery. We'll buy a few high stools and create more customer space.

Mary charged across the kitchen and threw her arms around her *daed*. *"Danki."* She turned back toward Sarah. "Both of you."

Danki, Lord Jesus, for touching Daed's heart so he could find a little money to spare. Mary glanced at the recipe and crushed it to her heart. Change was coming, and Mr. Noah Miller would soon discover that.

On Monday morning after getting his assistant squared away with her duties, Noah headed out the front door. A banging noise pulled his attention to the other side of the street. Was that racket coming from Sweet Delights?

Mary stepped out of her bakery, crossed

the street and walked past his store, giving him the silent treatment.

"Nice morning for a stroll, Mary. Business must be good."

She waved a hand in the air.

"What's all that noise? Workmen at your bakery?"

She stopped and turned. "Smucker's Electric is adding more outlets, and Bender Building and Supply is adding a luncheon counter."

He hadn't figured she'd remodel. "That's good. You must be planning on winning the contest next month?"

"Worried, Miller?"

"Nope. Actually, I was going to pay my grandparents a visit and try to get to know them better. I wasn't going to stay long, but I thought since you're Amish, your presence might serve as a buffer between us. If you wouldn't mind riding along, and I'm sure grandma would like your company."

Mary glanced back at Sweet Delights. "I can get my mail later. Let me run and tell

Amanda, but I can't be gone more than an hour or so."

"That's fine."

When she returned, Noah held the door for Mary while she slid in then ran around to his side. He started the engine and headed out of town. "How's the recipe for the festival coming along?"

"So that's why you asked me along?"

"Of course not. I thought if my grandparents see you, they might be nicer to me." That wasn't exactly the whole reason, but he couldn't tell her that.

"Noah, what did you expect?" She softened her tone. "It was your parents' decision to stay away." She reached across the console and laid a gentle hand on his arm. "Please try to understand it from their point of view."

"Yes, I realize that."

The next mile was quiet as Mary stared out her side window. She glanced his way, and he turned slightly to steal a look at her blond hair. Her cornflower-blue eyes set his heart ticking so hard he was afraid she'd hear it. He'd fibbed to her. He didn't need her as a buffer between him and his grandparents, he just wanted to enjoy sitting beside her. She was lovely.

"This is the place." Mary's voice brought him out of his musing.

"Thanks, I wasn't paying attention." He pulled in the drive and parked by the house.

She leaned in. "Are you nervous about seeing your *grosseldre* again?"

Slowly, he turned toward her. "In a way, my family is such a mystery to me. They're kin, yet they're strangers. But I want to know them, see them and feel like I'm part of their family."

She smiled. "So you're thinking about converting to Amish?"

"No, I don't really see me driving around in a buggy, going without electricity and dressing like everyone else in the community."

She eyed his plaid shirt then dropped her

gaze to his tan trousers. "*Jah*, I imagine Plain clothes wouldn't really be your style."

The barn door opened, and Thomas Miller walked in their direction.

Noah stepped out of his vehicle and opened the back door. "Mary, I brought a box of fresh green vegetables and some baked goods. Would you mind carrying it in the haus?"

"Sure." She glanced at Thomas approaching and turned to Noah. "Be honest with him. Don't pretend to be a grandson then disappear from his life."

Mary's words weighed on his heart as he walked to meet his grandpa. Mixed feelings pulled at his resolve. He had a dream for his future and expanding his brand into Des Moines. Yet he had a yearning to know his family, and in some small way, be part of their lives.

As the old man approached, Noah held out his hand. "Good morning."

"*Morgen.* Did you come to help mend

fence or learn to milk a cow?" Grandpa's frown deepened, but he shook Noah's hand.

Noah wasn't sure, but it almost sounded like his grandpa had made a joke. "I stopped by to bring Grandma some vegetables and baked goods from the store, but if you need help, I'll gladly do what I can."

"Farming is hard work."

"I know that, but I'd like to work with you, learn about farming and understand why you love it."

Grandpa harrumphed. A deep line creased his forehead.

The old man's expression tore at Noah's heart. The frown lines in his grandpa's face pointed to uncertainty, and it clawed at Noah's innermost man to think he wasn't trusted. He didn't want to disappoint his grandpa. He wanted to be able to talk to him and love him freely. But was that even possible? Would the old man let him? "Would you show me around your farm?"

Grandpa's face turned to one of puzzlement and then relaxed. "*Jah*, I can do that.

Come, we'll start with the milking floor."
He showed Noah all around the milking
room and went through the procedures.

Noah walked beside Grandpa in silence,
Mary's words circling around in his head.
Be honest with him. That was the question.
Was he being honest with the old man or
was he being selfish?

Mary knocked on the door, and Anna
opened it with a surprised look.

"*Gut Morgen*, Anna." Mary stepped in
and set the box on the table. "Noah packed
some fresh vegetables and breads for you."

"So our grandson has paid us another
visit, and you came along. *Danki,* it's *gut*
to have company. Would you like a cup of
tea?"

"That would be nice."

"Is our grandson thinking about joining
our community?"

Mary caught her breath. "Anna, you'll
need to ask Noah that question. I can't answer for him."

Anna's eyes sparkled. "I thought maybe you were courting, and that would bring our family back together."

Her words startled Mary. "*Nein*. We are not courting."

Anna nodded with disappointment crossing her face.

Mary's chest ached for Anna. When Seth left, it ripped her heart in two and packed it with distrust. When he returned, it filled her with conflict. So she well imagined Anna's distress. Mary hadn't known that Anna and Thomas had a son Jeremiah. That's the way it was with the Amish. If a child left the community, he was out of their lives. Now, this elderly couple had to deal with the conflict again.

"Would you like to see my current quilt project, Mary?" Anna asked. "It's turning out lovely."

"Sure."

Anna led the way to the room with her stretching rack. "It's called a Prairie Star patchwork quilt."

"The fall colors are beautiful." Mary examined the stitching. "You do *gut* work, Anna."

"And how is your bakery business? I enjoy stopping there when I'm in town."

A door banged closed, and Anna headed for the kitchen with Mary falling into step behind her. Thomas was in the kitchen, pouring a cup of coffee.

He nodded at Mary. "Noah is waiting for you by his vehicle."

"*Danki.* It was nice seeing you both." She hurried outside and down the walk. Noah held open the door, and she slid onto the seat. "What happened?"

Noah started the engine, drove down the drive and turned onto the gravel road. "He showed me around, starting with the milking floor and explained the procedure. Then he told me I should be learning this from my father. He reminded me that he was Amish, and I'm *Englisch.*"

Mary stared straight ahead. Thomas had politely drawn the line for Noah. It was a warning for him...that each should stay in their rightful community.

A twinge plucked at her heart. *Jah*, she too needed to take care and not spend too much time with Noah. He was *Englisch* and nothing could become of their friendship. She glanced his way as a hollow spot notched in her heart.

Chapter Ten

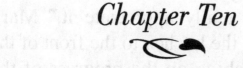

Tuesday at 9:00 a.m., Mary held open the front door of the bakery as Glenn and his *sohn* from Bender Building and Supply carried in the Formica countertop she wanted installed as a bar for stools.

"*Morgen*, Mary. We should be done by the end of the day. Pete's coming to do the electrical work, jah?"

"He promised he would be here today." A knock sounded on the back door. "Excuse me, Glenn."

She hurried to the kitchen and opened the back door. "*Morgen*, Pete. Glenn just asked if you were going to make it."

Pete set his Smuckers Electrical toolbox on the kitchen floor. "Sorry, I'm a little late, forgot something and had to run back to the shop and fetch it. But don't worry, the additional outlets should all be installed by the end of the day."

"*Danki*, I really appreciate it." Mary moved from the kitchen to the front of the bakery, checking on the progress of the countertop.

When convinced the men could handle things without her, Mary poured a cup of coffee and retreated to the office. She pulled out the bookkeeping ledger and journal and started catching up on bookwork. After three hours of nonstop work, she closed the books. The bottom line showed an increase in revenue. She was glad of that, but income still needed to be higher.

Mary wandered from her office into the front of the bakery and set her cup down. As her gaze swept the room, her jaw dropped open. The mounted counter fit perfectly under the windows. It was lovely and functional. The brown Formica matched the wooden stools. Hopefully, it would attract young customers to stop in for a cappuccino or latte.

Glenn pushed the front door open, set a box on the floor and began to fill it with scraps of wood and countertop. "It'll look better when I have the sawdust cleaned up and the stools unboxed and pushed under the counter."

"It looks *wunderbaar.*" She walked around to get a better look. "Don't worry about the sawdust. Jacob is going to help me clean and paint tomorrow. I'm just pleased you could work us into your schedule so fast."

"Glad to do it."

"Do I write a check now?"

"*Nein.* I have to add it all up and send you an invoice. We'll finish up and be out of your hair."

Pete poked his head around the kitchen doorjamb into the bakery. "I'm done. I'll total and send an invoice."

"*Danki*, Pete." Mary followed him to the

kitchen and ran her gaze around. "The extra outlets look *gut*. It's going to be great having them. And the generator that powers the bakery's electricity will be large enough to handle the extra outlets?"

"No problem, it's big enough."

After Pete gathered his toolbox and left, Mary headed back to the front of the bakery for one last walk through. She flicked the light switch, hitched King and steered him for home.

The peaceful clip-clop of horse's hooves on the road was soothing. Mary leaned back in the seat and let King set his gait to an easy trot. A new sensation bloomed in her chest. The old bakery was her *stiefmutter* Sarah's, but the newly decorated bakery was her idea. And even though the changes were minor, it made the shop feel like hers.

She clutched the string of her prayer *kapp* and twirled it around her finger. *Jah*, she would definitely have to confess that outburst of self-satisfaction and pride at what she'd done for the bakery. But who could blame her? It was finally happening! Her bakery was getting a new face.

King turned into the drive and headed for the barn. She unhitched the buggy, wiped King down and filled his oat and water pails. His brown eyes widened with anticipation. She patted his mane and closed the barn door behind her. She carried her quilted bag to the *haus* and hung it on a peg by the door.

Her *stiefmutter* turned from the sink. "You're home. How did it go today?"

"*Wunderbaar.* It looks great. I can't wait until Jacob and I get it painted tomorrow."

Jacob banged the screen door closed. "What am I going to get out of all this work?"

Mary ran over to him and mussed his hair. "I'll make you my contest apple pie and you can eat the whole thing."

He chuckled. "I'm going to hold you to that."

The screen door squeaked open and *Daed*

wiped his shoes on the rag rug. "What's going on in here?"

"I was telling them the additional outlets and the new counter were installed today and it all looks *wunderbaar*." Mary gave *Daed* a kiss on the cheek. *"Danki."*

"Gut, I'm glad to hear it. Do you think it will help keep the bakery open?" His tone laced with skepticism.

Mary took a step back. *"Daed*, it sounds like you don't believe I can do it?"

"Nein. I didn't mean that. You are a terrific baker, and you can do whatever you set your mind to do. I'm only saying that Noah's store also has fresh vegetables, a nice deli and delicious baked goods."

"And how do you know how his food tastes?" she huffed.

Silence loomed across the kitchen.

Jacob shoved his hands in his pocket. "If *Daed* and I are hungry when we're in town, Noah's deli is a convenient place to grab a quick sandwich or a slice of pizza. His tuna sandwiches are super, and I don't care much for tuna fish."

"So you go behind my back and sneak off to the competition." Her voice strained. "And what do you think of his breads and pastries, are they *gut*?"

Jacob glanced at *Daed*. "*Jah*, his pastries are *gut*. His pecan pie is better than yours."

Mary gasped. "You're just saying that."

"Sorry, sis, but I'm telling the truth." Jacob reached up and pulled a string on her prayer *kapp*. "You better practice for that baking contest, because you're going to need all the practice you can get. Have you tried his baking? His croissants are the best I've ever had."

Mary turned toward *Daed*. "Is that what you think, too?"

Daed nodded.

Mary pulled a chair away from the table and sat. "*Mamm*, I had no idea."

Sarah wrapped her arms around Mary. "We'll work on some recipes. You'll see. We'll come up with some delicious new ones."

Horses' hooves tromped up the drive, and buggy wheels skidded to a stop. *Daed* stepped to the door and walked out on the porch.

A minute later, he burst back into the kitchen. "The bakery is on fire. Let's get to town."

"I'll stay here with the *kinner*," *Mamm* yelled. "Mary, you and Jacob go. Hurry!"

"Mary, get your things. Jacob and I'll hitch the buggy," *Daed* shouted on his way out the door.

Mary paced the ground until the buggy pulled up to the *haus* with both Tidbit and King hitched. She jumped in the back seat.

Daed shook the reins. "Hee-yah!" The horses jerked the buggy and tore off down the driveway. *Daed* slowed them to turn onto the road then headed to town. He tapped the reins again. "Hee-yah."

Mary twisted her hands on her quilted bag handles so hard her fingers hurt. "Go faster, *Daed*."

"*Jah*, I'm trying to do that, but others use

the road too. The firemen are there taking care of it."

"I know, but I want to see what's happening." The three miles to town seemed endless to Mary.

Arriving at the edge of town, the air reeked of burnt wood. When the buggy drew closer, toxic fumes from the fire stung Mary's eyes. As the building came into view, she scooted to the end of the seat, threw her hands to her mouth and gasped. *Daed* stopped outside the barricades. Firetrucks, police cars and red lights filled the street in front of the bakery.

Mary sniffled as tears filled her eyes and drenched her cheek. *"Nein, nein."* Flames still engulfed the inside of the building as hoses spayed water from all sides. *"Nein."* She threw herself back against the seat. "Oh, *nein, Mamm* is going to be devastated."

She slipped her hand in her bag, scratched around and pulled out a handkerchief. She wiped the tears off her cheeks and blew her nose.

Daed turned King and Tidbit around. "I'm going to get the horses away from here. We'll walk back and get closer." He parked in a lot a block away.

Jacob opened the door, Mary jumped out, and they walked toward the destruction. Her body was numb, her legs almost unwilling to take another step. She stopped in front of Noah's store and watched the smoldering building from the other side of the street outside the police barricades.

Thirty minutes later, firefighters still shouted to each other and aimed hoses at the dying flames. Noah stood in his yellow Nomex gear beside something they'd taken from the burning building. Black char clung to the sides, so Mary couldn't make out the object.

Daed stepped closer and wrapped his arm around her shoulders. "Are you okay?"

"*Jah*, but even seeing it, I'm still in disbelief."

He squeezed her to his side.

Mary drew a deep breath with sobs catching in her throat. "Can we rebuild right away?"

Her vater patted her arm. "We'll have to talk to Sarah and see what she wants to do."

Mayor Conrad walked up behind *Daed* and patted him on the back. "Sorry about the bakery, Caleb. We need your business in town, so I hope you decide to rebuild."

"*Danki*, Mr. Conrad. It's just such a shock. Something we never expected to happen."

"We're all praying for your family. I'm going to go over and talk to the fire chief. Take care, Caleb." Mayor Conrad turned and faced Mary. "It's a real shame, but rebuild." He nodded, then headed across the street.

Jacob shuffled his feet around on the sidewalk, trying to get a better look. "*Daed*, I'm going to go over and talk with Noah Miller and see if the firemen know where the fire started."

Daed nodded. "They might not know yet, but I'll walk with you."

They crossed the street, staying out of the

firefighters' way. When Noah had his hands free, Jacob approached him and they talked for a minute. After a few more moments, Jacob and Daed walked closer to the building where the chief was, but Noah turned and headed toward Mary.

He stopped beside her and turned back to look at the charred building. "How ya doing, Mary? Sorry about Sweet Delights." He stumbled over each word in a soft voice.

Tears blurred her eye. "Now you're the only bakery in town." Her voice quaked and tears streamed down her face. "I'll never get my business back."

His amber gaze of concern met and held hers. "You'll rebuild." He stepped closer, as if trying to lend her his strength should she need it.

"Amish don't have insurance. By the time we find the money, which I doubt *Daed* could do, everyone would be used to shopping at your store."

"Don't underestimate your loyal customers. Sure, they might like something I sell, pizza, a favorite sandwich, but they still love Sweet Delights."

Her chest ached, her eyes felt puffy, and her face was wet with a continuous stream of tears. "The mainstay of my life has been ripped from me. Even if we can rebuild, it won't be the same place that Sarah's *daed* started. His soul filled those four walls. Customers remember all the *gut* times they had there, his recipes, his joking with them. He helped the community, and they loved him. Most of his recipes were just destroyed."

"Did you have his recipe book locked in a safe? The fire burned at 1,100 degrees Fahrenheit." He softened his voice. "There won't be much, if anything salvageable. The book would have burned."

She gulped a breath as her life was tearing into pieces at his news. "Jah, I locked the recipe book in the safe, along with the ledger and journal." She sobbed. "Now everything is gone."

Why, Gott...why? I have nothing to my

name. I loved Sarah's bakery, and You took that. I don't even have my quilt anymore.*

Noah wrapped an arm around her shoulders and pulled her close, so close she could feel his breath on her cheek. "Shh, Mary. Sometimes God takes away so He can give us something better." His words wrapped around her like a prayer. "It might not be much, but the safe survived the fire. It's smoldering now, but we had the hot fire put out in forty-five minutes. I'll have it moved to my store for safekeeping, if you want."

Mary sniffled and swallowed hard. "*Jah*, that would be fine."

A protective twinge tightened Noah's throat as he glanced down at Mary, snuggling close to his chest. "Do you want to come inside my store to sit and rest?"

"*Danki*, but I want to go home." She blotted a tear running down her cheek. "*Mamm* will be a wreck wanting to know what's going on. It was her *vater's* bakery, and it meant a lot to her. It will just devastate her. And I need to stop and tell Amanda."

"Mary, I can't tell you how sorry I am."

"Don't talk, Noah. My heart was just ripped out, and I don't want to discuss it. Not right this minute, I can't."

He drew in a ragged breath and nodded. He released his arm. "Listen, we aren't enemies. I never meant to hurt you or drive you out of business. I'm truly sorry I put my store across from Sweet Delights. When I rented the building, I knew there was a drug store on one side and an antique store on the other, but I didn't check the whole street. I'll give you space in my store, and you can keep your bakery going. You can use my ovens and whatever else you need until your shop is rebuilt."

Mary's eyes widened. "What? I couldn't possibly do that. Have you lost your senses?"

Noah smiled and shook his head. "Of course not, but thanks for asking. Everyone in town knows we're competing, and I don't want them to think I'd take advantage of you after your bakery burned. Someone might even say I started it."

Mary jerked her head up and locked eyes with him. "No one in this town would ever accuse you of that."

"It could start as a joke and get around. That would ruin my reputation, and it would be your fault for not working with me and squashing any loose gossip."

"Mr. Miller, you have a way of exaggerating the problem." She shook her head with a smirk.

"Yeah, but what do you say? I'd sure feel better about everything if you would let me help you."

Mary drew a deep breath of smelly, smoky, toxic air, coughed and stepped back. She glanced across the street at the smoldering building. "I don't know how long it will take to rebuild, or if *Daed* and *Mamm* will want to." Tears filled her eyes and clung to her lashes. She batted them away.

"We don't have to talk about length of time now. Moving a small part of your baking to my store is only a temporary situation. Unless you would rather come and work for me?"

"Not even as a joke. Then people probably would think you did it on purpose to get me to bake for you since your baking tastes terrible." A smile pulled at the corners of her mouth.

"I know it's a big decision, Mary. Take your time."

As she stared at her bakery, or what was left of it, he watched the change of emotions cross her face. What would it be like working side by side with her every day?

She turned and opened her mouth as if she was going to say something but then hesitated...

His heart drummed up into his throat, so hard he couldn't speak. He wanted her to say yes, but would she?

Chapter Eleven

Heat worked its way up Mary's neck and burned her ears. She couldn't move her bakery to Noah's store. It was an outrageous suggestion.

It was a solution, but one she abhorred. She couldn't sell her baked goods out of Noah's store, and she certainly didn't want to see him on a daily basis.

She couldn't work with an *Englischer*. What would her community think? Her *Gmay* frowned on a member having a partnership with an *Englischer*. Of course, it wouldn't be a real partnership, but others might not see it that way. And the bishop had warned her more than once about getting too close to Noah.

Not to mention, working that close to Noah would make it impossible for her to stay clear of him. All the reasons why she shouldn't agree.

Noah cleared his throat. "Do you want to think it over?"

She shook her head and faced him. "*Nein.* I don't think it would work." She glanced across the street at the charred remains of Sweet Delights and already regretted her decision.

"You know it could take a year to get your bakery rebuilt."

She straightened her back. "Why are you trying to talk me into it? Do you want me to show you how to bake really *gut* pastries? Is that it?"

"Oh, so you think I need your recipes?" He laughed. "I'm just trying to be nice."

"All right, Noah. I'll move my bakery to a small corner of your store and try to keep my customers that have a standing order.

But this is only temporary, just for a few weeks. Could I put a small sign in your window?"

He hesitated but nodded. "I have a storage room that's large enough for a small office to fit a desk and your safe. I'll clear a corner of the store tomorrow."

"*Danki.* That's very nice of you and it gives me time to visit a kitchen supply shop in Iowa City to pick up a few of my favorite utensils and bowls."

"I'd be glad to take you. The SUV's got plenty of room for hauling whatever you need."

Mary shook her head. "I couldn't ask you to take time away from your work. You're already doing enough for me."

"I need to pick up a few things. You can ride along."

She eyed him curiously. "You act like you feel guilty that my bakery burned."

He paused and looked across the street. "No, it's not guilt. It's empathy." Emotion caught in his throat. "When both of my parents died at once in the car accident, the store was all I had for security, and my sisters looked up to me to take care of them. I don't know what I would have done if I'd lost the store, too. It would have been like losing my parents all over again."

Mary touched his arm, large tears blocking her vision.

He shuffled his booted feet. "I want to do this. I know how much it hurts, and I want to help."

"You make me feel like I can't turn down your offer. And I wouldn't know what to do with myself if I didn't get up in the *morgen* and bake." She raised her chin. "I'm sure we can work together…at least for a little while until I figure things out."

She turned toward the street as *Daed's* buggy pulled up next to the curb. "Ready to go, Mary? Your *mamm* will be waiting to hear the news, and there is nothing more we can do here."

Noah raised a hand and squeezed her shoulder. "I'll pick you up at 9:00 a.m., and we'll go to the supply store in Iowa City. We can come back and get you settled in your office. After that, we can clear a spot in the bakery and set up a table or two for your baked goods. It'll be a snug fit, but I think we can manage. While you're here, I'll do my baking over at the other store. I mostly do that anyway."

"That sounds great. *Danki*, Noah."

Mary climbed in the buggy and sat on the back seat behind Jacob. She took one last glance at Sweet Delights and pain knifed its way through her heart. She had a lot to think about. Could she work next to Noah when he was the competition?

She leaned back in the seat. *Jah*, it was nice that Noah had invited her to use a corner of his store. It would allow her to keep some of her customers. On the other hand, now her customers would get used to shopping at Noah's store.

She needed to win the baking contest now more than ever, and she needed to keep her distance from Noah. But were either of those even possible?

Wednesday morning, the bright sunlight poured into Mary's bedroom, startling her awake. She jerked upright in bed and glanced out the window at a few fluffy clouds racing across the blue sky. Her heart thumped as her memory rekindled last night's disaster. She forced herself to take a deep breath.

Yawning, she sat and stretched. *Mamm* had let her sleep after a long night of talking and crying.

She glanced at the clock. *Ach*, Noah would arrive soon to take her to the kitchen supply store. She jumped out of bed, dressed and hurried downstairs. When she stepped into the kitchen, *Mamm* was flipping pancakes. "Morgen."

"*Morgen*, sweetheart."

"*Danki* for fixing my favorite breakfast. I feel like you are trying to comfort me, but you lost a bakery, too."

"*Nein*, I felt bad because it belonged to *Daed*, but I hardly spend any time there now. My life won't change much that it's gone."

"What do you think of me having a corner of my bakery in Noah's store? You never really answered me last night."

Sarah turned from the stove and faced Mary. "It was nice of him to make that offer. It probably wouldn't hurt for a little while."

After breakfast, Mary hurried and washed dishes, and was just finishing when Noah pulled into the driveway. She grabbed her bag and ran for the door. "I'm leaving, *Mamm*."

She climbed into the SUV, closed the door and buckled up. "*Morgen*, Noah."

"Good morning." He drove down the gravel road, turned onto Route 218 and headed for Iowa City. "You should have taken a couple of days off, even the rest of the week."

"*Danki* for the suggestion, but I think it's better if I fight my fear and keep going. If

I give in to it, fear wins. This is a test, and I will persevere."

"Your faith seems to be lifting you up."

She faced Noah. "I think if I keep my hands busy, it will keep my mind off the horror of my situation."

Noah could smell the subtle fragrance of lavender from Mary's soap. Intoxicating. The profile of her delicate features, her blond hair and creamy complexion sent his heart into overdrive. He took a deep breath and tried to clear his head.

He kept his eyes on the road, and she seemed content to watch the scenery. The sky had cleared to a robin's-egg blue, and it was a beautiful day for a ride.

At the supply store in Iowa City, Noah parked his vehicle and escorted her inside. He watched her eyes light up with curiosity when they walked by all the electrical appliances. She stopped and read an ad for an air fryer, then turned to Noah. "Do you have one of these?"

"Yes, I like it. No grease and it reduces calories by seventy-five percent. It's very healthy cooking."

She moved around until she came to the fancy espresso machines. "I'd like to have one of these for my shop one day."

While he followed, Mary moved on to the glassware section and placed a three-piece bowl set in her shopping cart.

Continuing on to the bakeware area, she looked at the easy-release nonstick pans. "Sweet Delights had pans that were fifty years old, maybe older. Now, I'll need to buy all new." Her voice hitched.

Noah patted her shoulder. "Look at it this way, your new pans will give you inspiration to develop new recipes."

She gave a weak smile. "Maybe."

He gave her back a pat. "You okay?"

She nodded.

"If you want to wander around by yourself, I can meet you at the small appliance in thirty minutes? Or we can stay together?"

"Jah, I'd like to walk around by myself and just look."

He picked up what he needed then met Mary at the small appliances. She was looking at a panini grill and a triple slow cooker.

"I have one of those," he commented. "The three cookers come in handy."

She glanced around. "I could stay in here all day. I never knew some of these contraptions existed."

Noah laughed. "This store is a cook's dream come true."

When they reached the checkout line, he motioned for her to push her cart ahead of him. She placed her bakeware, bowls, set of cutlery and a large iron skillet on the counter and paid with a check.

Noah paid for his filters, bread pans and bakeware, then set his plastic sacks in Mary's cart. He pushed the cart out to his SUV and loaded their supplies in the back.

She settled into the passenger seat and buckled the seat belt. "We never really got into specifics last night. Exactly what did you have in mind? Do I bake for you in addition to baking for my own business, or am I renting the space and the use of your ovens? And how much would that cost?"

Noah jerked as he buckled into his own seat. "Whoa, slow down. That's too many questions."

"*Nein*, I want to settle it now." She raised her chin.

"I thought we could work it out. I'm not charging any rent. You can bake for your regular weekly orders, and I'll set up a display case for you to sell a few extras, whatever you want. But it won't be a big area. I don't have a lot of extra space."

She rubbed her hand across the edge of the dash then laid it back in her lap. "I was thinking I could rent the space and pay whatever amount you thought fair for using your ovens. I'll put a small pantry in my office if you want me to keep my supplies separate. If you're going to bake in the kitchen, I'll need a schedule of when I can use the ovens." She glanced toward Noah.

He met her gaze for a second then started his vehicle.

"I don't want charity, Noah."

He ran his knuckles across his jaw. "I'll need to think about what to charge you. I'll figure out the square footage and charge accordingly. Let me run some numbers, and I can let you know tomorrow." He hadn't really thought about all the particulars. This could get complicated, and he didn't just mean with the baking arrangement. He liked her, really liked her.

"I want to bake for my regulars in your store, but I ache inside like a piece of me has been cut out. Do you know what I mean?" Her voice wobbled.

"Yes, I know all too well."

She sat in silence. He glanced at her and saw tears pooled in her eyes. Her cheeks were pale. She was no doubt worried sick and in no shape to work, but he understood the need to keep hands busy. It had worked for him when his parents died.

When they reached his store in Kalona, he

gave her a tour of the layout and the kitchen. He cleared spots in his cupboards and in the pantry for her supplies.

Mary nodded. "My heart feels as empty as those shelves you cleared for me."

She asked questions in a voice fighting for control. He could see this was the last place she wanted to be. It probably irked her that her competition was going to be right under her nose watching every move she made.

Noah gulped. This might be the worst decision he'd ever made.

When Jenny called Noah into the office to discuss an urgent matter, Mary took the opportunity to walk through his store by herself. She looked at every item in his bakery. Her eyes widened at her discovery. She offered similar products at her bakery, except his portions were smaller and cheaper than a serving at Sweet Delights. She hadn't noticed that when she toured his store on opening day. Now she got it when Emily had told her that Noah called her heavy-handed when she cut portions.

She glanced at the office door, still closed. She headed for the kitchen to give it a better examination than what Noah's whirlwind tour offered. A woman was there baking.

"*Hallo*, I'm Mary. I might be working here for a while."

She nodded. "I'm Jean Dwyer. Noah told me you'd be working here. It's nice to meet you. Sorry to hear about your bakery." Jean was lovely and very petite. Maybe thirty.

"*Danki*, it's nice to meet you, too."

When Jean left the room to take a tray of cupcakes to the front, Mary snatched a mini cupcake and popped it in her mouth. She shook her head in disbelief. "Mmm." It was maybe one of the best cupcakes she'd ever eaten.

Shame prickled her skin with goose bumps at sneaking the treat. She'd given Noah and his sisters a free treat. Therefore, she could reciprocate. She wasn't quite sure Bishop Yoder would see it that way. But if she was going to work here, no doubt she and Noah would be trying each other's products. Except for their contest entries of course.

She bit into a chocolate cookie and stopped chewing to savor the taste. It was delicious.

Now more than ever, she knew she needed that prize money.

Chapter Twelve

On Monday, while Mary used his kitchen, Noah loaded his SUV with a box of vegetables, breads and pastries. He stopped and picked up Emily at her friend, Kate's, house, and they headed to his grandparents' farm.

"Noah, I don't know them. What do I say to grandma?" Emily worried her bottom lip.

"You can talk about the store and what you do to help. Ask Grandma about her life on the farm." For the rest of the ride, he could tell by her fidgeting and kicking legs that Emily was concerned about meeting her grandparents.

Pulling into the driveway, Noah glanced

around the barnyard, his grandpa wasn't anywhere in sight. He parked by the house, gave the lighter box with bread and rolls to Emily and carried the other two boxes to the house.

Just as they reached the steps, Uncle Cyrus drove a horse and hayrack up the drive and stopped by the SUV. Cyrus stepped down and shot Noah a stern look.

Noah entered the house and set his boxes in the kitchen. "Grandma," he called, "I brought you veggies and bread. Emily came with me to keep you company."

Grandma hurried into the kitchen from the other room. "*Danki*, Noah. Come in, Emily. I'm glad you came. Your cousins will be here later, and you can meet them." She glanced at Noah. "We'll be fine."

Noah stepped off the porch and met Cyrus halfway.

"My *daed* is in the north forty bailing straw. You should have gotten here earlier so you could have helped him."

Noah straightened his back. "I'm here now."

"Why? Your father never cared. Why do you?"

"Cyrus, I can't remedy what my father did. I'm sorry he didn't like the farm. Nothing will change that now. But I'd like to help whenever I can."

Cyrus squared his shoulders. "Your *daed*, my *bruder*, was helping *Daed* shingle the barn roof. Jeremiah went into town for more shingles and was gone too long. *Daed* fell off the roof and lay on the ground a long time before anyone found him. It's Jeremiah's fault *Daed* walks with a cane. It would be better if you didn't hang around too much and get the old man's hopes up. You aren't part of our community. Why are you here?"

"Because I want to help my grandparents and to get to know them."

"You have a store to take care of, and farming is a full-time job."

"He's an old man, and he needs all the help he can get, even if it's just temporary.

Instead of talking, let's go to the field and give him a hand."

Cyrus nodded and motioned for Noah to climb onto the hayrack. When they reached the field where his grandpa was baling, his uncle showed Noah how to grab the bales and stack them.

As the afternoon wore on, Noah stacked hundred-pound bales one after the other until blisters formed on his palms even with gloves. Dust filled the air and clung to his sweaty face and clothing. He coughed and swiped his mouth with his shirtsleeve.

Cyrus pulled the bandana from his neck and handed it to Noah. Noah wrapped it over his nose and mouth and tied it behind his head. The chaff irritated his neck, and worked its way down inside his shirt. He gritted his teeth but kept on stacking until they finished the baling.

When they reached the barnyard, Noah jumped off the hayrack. His feet were tired and wobbled.

Grandpa smiled and slapped him on the

back. "After we eat, you better go home and take care of those hands. *Danki* for the help."

Noah nodded. He could see by the tears shining in his grandpa's eyes that he appreciated the help a whole lot more than he expressed.

After dinner, Noah helped Emily in the car. "Did you enjoy meeting your cousins?"

"Yes, we had a great time. They showed me how to knit." For the next three miles to town, Emily told him all about her cousins and what she'd learned.

Noah parked behind his store and slowly stepped out. After sitting for a while, his body was so stiff he could hardly move. He was tired, but his heart was full.

Tuesday morning, Mary headed to Amanda's *haus* in Kalona. The front door opened, and Amanda hurried to the buggy. She stepped in and slid onto the seat.

"*Danki* for stopping by yesterday and asking me to come and help. *Mamm* finished canning, and I was getting bored. Saturday, I helped my friend at the newspaper get out some flyers. So spill, Mary, how is it working with Noah?"

"It's been a week since Sweet Delights burned, and so far, it's working. He goes out to his grandpa's farm sometimes, and he helps bake at the other store so we're not in the kitchen at the same time. But today, I want to practice my contest entry and thought you could make a dozen loaves of bread and six dozen rolls for our regular customers while I do that. I don't want to lose them to Noah."

"I'm glad to help."

Mary parked the buggy, unhitched King, then gave Amanda the tour of the kitchen layout. Having her friend by her side once again made her decision to bake at Noah's store seem normal. "I'll show you Sweet Delight's corner of the store. I'm so grateful he gave me the space."

She showed Amanda her pantry and settled her at her station in the kitchen.

Mary scooted to the pantry for her ingredients, mixed the practice dough, and set the rolls to rise.

Jean Dwyer flew through the swinging door like an unruly child. "Hello everyone I was almost late."

"And, Amanda, this is Jean Dwyer, Noah's assistant. Jean, this is Amanda Stutzman. She's going to be helping me with the baking while I spend time practicing my recipes for the contest."

"Welcome, Amanda," Jean responded with a smile. "I bake a few things here for Noah and watch the store."

"It's nice to meet you, Jean."

Later in the morning, Noah bumped the kitchen door open, carrying in a box of baked goods, but stopped when he saw Amanda. "Good morning, ladies. Smells like you two have been busy."

"We wanted to have most of our baking done before you and Jean get busy," Mary motioned to her full bakery rack.

"What is that apple dessert you're making? It looks good. Can I have a sample?" he said, teasingly.

"Not from this one. It's my practice for the contest."

He walked to the counter, leaned over and took a long sniff. "Your pie smells like it might be hard to beat." His tone was serious. "Your cupcakes look good, too. Can I have one of those?"

She nodded. "Be my guest."

He took a bite. "They're good." He let a smirk play on his lips. "But mine are better."

Amanda laughed. "Mary's chocolate cupcakes are delicious."

He countered, "Try one of mine. Let's go out to the bakery. You can each have one."

Mary followed Noah and Amanda to the store's bakery section. The three of them weaved their way around Mrs. Wallin browsing the cakes.

Amanda selected a chocolate cupcake, pulled the paper back and took a bite. "Mmm." She held it out to Mary. "This is really *gut*."

Mary took a bite. "I don't know. I think mine are better." A wry smile pulled at her mouth.

Mrs. Wallin moved closer. "Why don't you have a contest on Saturday? You can both bake those mini cupcakes and let the customers do a blind taste test."

Noah whistled. "Oh, I like that idea. That will bring customers into the store." He raised a brow. "What do you think, Mary?"

She hadn't expected this. It was sort of a pre-contest test to see what others think. "Amanda, could you have your friend put a write-up in the newspaper? Maybe say from opening until closing on Saturday, you're invited to Miller's Farm-fresh Grocery, Delicatessen and Bakery for a free mini cupcake taste-testing between Miller's bakery and the Amish Sweet Delight's bakery and voting for the best one."

"If Noah agrees to it," Amanda said, "I'll write it up and take it over to the newspaper right now."

Mary stammered, "I think we should also

make the same kind of cupcake—chocolate, vanilla or whatever we decide."

Noah rubbed his hand across his chin. "Agreed. How about strawberry?"

"I'll agree to that." Mary tried to hide the smile pulling at her mouth. Strawberry cupcakes were one of her specialties.

Saturday just before 7:00 a.m., Mary set the last of her cupcakes on a bakery cart. Noah rolled both his cart and hers, each loaded with strawberry cupcakes, to the front of the store. One cart labeled A, the other B.

Mary followed him to the front and set paper and pencils next to a locked drum with a slit in the top. She opened a package of napkins and laid them on the counter next to the carts.

After Noah unlocked the front doors and headed off to stock the fresh lettuce, Mary watched the supply of cupcakes closely as she worked around the Sweet Delights area.

She swept the floor often to clean up the

littered cupcake papers and crumbs. There was laughing and whispering, but Mary kept far enough away so she wouldn't overhear the customers' discussions.

She grabbed an empty tray from the cart and stopped by checkout where Jean was working. "There's a good turnout for voting."

Jean smiled. "Yes, did you see the write-up in the newspaper about the contest?" She pulled it from below the counter and handed it to Mary, already open to the article.

Mary scanned the headline and gasped.
Cupcake Bake-off Between Dueling Bakeries
Setting the baking pan on the counter, she snapped the newspaper closed and hustled across the store to the produce section where Noah was restocking. She shook the paper. "Did you see the article about our little contest?"

He paused and faced her. "No, I've been too busy."

"The newspaper is calling it *dueling bakeries*."

He shrugged. "That's sort of what it is, don't you think?"

She huffed, then trotted back across the store and handed the newspaper back to Jean. She grabbed the empty pan, took it to the kitchen, and brought another tray to the front. It seemed the whole town had turned out for their little contest.

In the late afternoon, Emily dashed across the bakery and hugged Mary.

Mary squeezed her tightly. "Where have you been? I haven't seen you in days."

"I have a girlfriend, her name is Kate. We're in third grade together, and I go over to her house to play."

"That's *gut*. How do you like your classes?"

"They're great." Emily eyed the contest sign then turned toward the cupcakes. "Can I have a cupcake and vote?"

"Of course."

Emily ate cupcake A first, then B. "Mmm.

They're both good." She took a slip of paper and a pencil, voted and stuffed it in the drum. She turned back to Mary. "Can I help you count the votes when it's all over?"

"Sorry, sweetie. Milton Accounting is going to count the votes, and they'll put the results in the morning's newspaper."

The store's door opened, and a local news team filed into the bakery with a camera and microphone.

Emily squealed, "Are we going to be on TV?"

Mary froze as her heart dropped to her stomach. "I don't know why they're here."

The reporter with the Channel 4 logo on his blue blazer weaved his way around the lines of people testing cupcakes and voting. He stepped forward. "Are you Mary Brenneman?"

She pulled her frame up to full stature. "Can I help you?"

"You're the owner of Sweet Delights bakery?"

Mary clenched her moist palms. "*Jah*,

what's this all about?" Her gaze bounced from the reporter to the cameraperson filming the people in line.

"I'm Carl Thompson, Channel 4 News. Someone called in on the tip line. We also saw the article about the dueling bakeries and contest to determine the best cupcake."

Annoyance inched its way up Mary's back. If she lost the contest, they would report it in the newspaper and on Channel 4 News for everyone to hear and gossip about. She hadn't thought about that when she agreed to this contest. She took a step back.

Noah's heavy footfalls approached from the kitchen. "What's going on here?"

Mary swung around. "Someone called Channel 4 and told them we were dueling bakeries."

"Is that what they said?"

"Someone called them on the tip line."

Carl butted in, "We also heard that you've both entered the Kalona Fall Apple Festival baking contest. They said you decided to have a cupcake contest first to raise the stakes between the two of you and put pressure on the loser."

Mary gasped. "I can't believe you would stoop so low to call a news channel, Noah."

"Roll camera," Carl told his videographer.

"Mary, I didn't do that." Noah turned to the reporter. "Who called you?"

"I'm sorry, it's an anonymous tip line. We don't know who called in. Apparently, everyone in this town knows what's going on between you two. We also heard you offered her a corner of your store after her bakery burned down. That's generous of you, Mr. Miller, one business owner helping another. Is that just until her bakery reopens?"

Mary plopped her hands on her hips as heat rushed to her cheeks.

"Mary, I'm not the one who called," Noah insisted. "Apparently, someone in town has a sense of humor."

"Or you thought it would make for great publicity when you won," she snarled.

Mayor Conrad pushed his way through

the gathering crowd. "I called Channel 4. I thought this would make great publicity for our fall festival."

Mary blew out a heavy sigh and glanced at the clock. "Just a reminder, everyone," she raised her voice, "the doors close in two minutes." She moved to the counter and began cleaning.

Noah held the front door open while the last of the voters streamed out, along with the mayor who was talking to the news crew about the festival. The last person to leave was from Milton Accounting, taking the locked drum of votes for counting in a secure room.

Noah locked the door and turned to Mary. "I'm sorry. This was probably a bad idea."

She stopped cleaning. "No, I apologize. I shouldn't have jumped on you. The only thing that ran through my mind was how embarrassed I'll be if I lose. I made a spectacle of myself, and now they have it on film. If the bishop hears about me being on TV, he'll discipline me."

"Mary, I'm so sorry. I didn't think about that. I'll contact the channel and tell them they can't put your image on TV." He darted back to the office.

In a few minutes, Noah returned to the front of the store, plugged in a small TV and got it ready for watching the ten o'clock news. He glanced her way. "I can drive you home tonight and pick you up in the morning so you don't have to drive King all the way home after dark."

"*Danki*, but I'm going to spend the night with Amanda and her folks." Mary gathered her cleaning supplies and wiped down her Sweet Delights area while Noah went back to his office.

At ten, Noah carried out two folding chairs and placed them in front of the TV. Mary sat on the edge of her seat, her back straight, praying. *Dear Lord, please don't let my image appear on the television for all to see.*

When the cupcake contest segment began, the news anchor brought out the representative from the accounting firm. They cut to a short clip showing the front of Noah's store, the locked drum and the people waiting in lines to eat cupcakes and vote. But neither Mary nor Noah were shown.

The accountant presented the envelope to the news anchor. A drum roll blasted through the TV speakers, and the anchor opened the envelope and gasped.

"Well, viewers, it seems there is a tie, and the duel will continue until the Kalona Fall Apple Festival baking contest on September 27. Will the winner be Mary Brenneman from the Amish Sweet Delights bakery, Noah Miller from Miller's Farm-fresh Grocery, Delicatessen and Bakery, or someone else entirely? May the best baker win."

One last film clip caught the reporter, Carl Thompson, eating a cupcake. Then they cut to the next segment.

Noah flipped the TV off.

"*Danki*, Noah." Her throat tightened around a lump that tried to block her words. "For asking them not to put my image on TV."

She enjoyed the way he looked after her… almost like they were a couple, and he really cared. She could trust him.

"I'll see you tomorrow." Mary walked out the back door, shutting it tightly, as if that could stop the brewing of happiness deep inside from overflowing. She liked Noah, maybe too much. She was Amish, and he was *Englisch*. Where could the relationship go?

Chapter Thirteen

Thursday dawned warm for a September morning. Mary arrived at Noah's store, tried the door, then pulled out her key and unlocked it. She wondered where everyone was. Noah was usually here by now.

She hung her bag and found a note from Noah stuck to the door.

In the kitchen, she grabbed a bag of apples from the cooler and peeled enough for two desserts. Humming a song from the *Ausbund*, she prepared a dumpling pastry, set it in a pie pan, spiced the apples with cinnamon, ginger and a little nutmeg, then poured them in the dish. She covered the top with woven strips and set it in the oven.

Sliding the new attic recipe in front of her, she prepared a pie shell, arranged the spiced apples in the pan, topped it with a crust and set it in the oven to bake. The secret to this pie was simmering the spices in apple juice and thickening the sauce before pouring it over the apples. Her contest entry would have to come from one of these two pies.

Amanda pushed the back door open. "I don't think I'll ever get used to coming to Noah's fancy kitchen in the morning."

Mary smiled. "I know what you mean."

"No one else is in yet?" Amanda bumped the bowls as she took them from the cupboard.

Mary grabbed the potholders, pulled her pies from the oven and set them on a rack to cool. "Jean will come in soon, but Noah left a note saying he went to Iowa City to bake. I think he wanted to practice his entry without me watching."

"That's *gut*." Amanda snorted as she

scooted to the pantry "Then he can't see our secrets either. Have you heard when or if your parents are going to rebuild Sweet Delights?" She mixed a batch of chocolate cupcakes and sugar cookies.

"*Nein, Daed* has to wait on crops to see if he has enough money. But even if he does, the bakery will have only the basics." Her voice dipped, "I still have to win the contest. My pies should be cool enough to eat. Let's try them before Noah returns."

While Amanda poured two glasses of water and pulled out forks, Mary cut two slices from each pie. She handed Amanda her plate.

Her friend took a bite of the dumpling pie first. "Mmm," she hummed and raised an eyebrow. She sipped water and tried the other piece. "Oh, Mary—" she pointed to the pie with her fork "—this second one is *wunderbaar*. What do you think?"

Mary tasted her revamped recipe of the dumpling pie with the cinnamon and nutmeg and caramel drizzle. The crust was delicious and flaky. It was going to be hard to beat. Her hand tightened around the fork. She glanced at Amanda then cut into the pie made from the attic recipe. She put it in her mouth and slowly chewed. "Bishop Ropp was right. I, too, would drive five miles for a piece of this pie. I've found my entry."

After finishing her pie, Mary cleaned the mess while Amanda carried her frosted cupcakes to the front of the bakery. When the sugar cookies Amanda had made were cool, Mary carted the tray to the front. She set it down and started to arrange the sweets in the display case.

Amanda stayed quiet, too quiet. Mary glanced at her friend working on the display case. "Is something wrong?"

"My *mamm* just stopped by for a moment." Amanda hesitated. "Did you know everyone in town is talking about your alleged feud, the cupcake-duel and the tie? She said people are saying it went *viral*."

Mary jerked her head toward Amanda. "What does that mean?"

"It means that people are sending notes out online for the world to see. *Mamm* said it's all over and everyone is talking about your feud with Noah and the upcoming festival."

The door pushed open, and Frank Wallin strolled to the counter. "Good morning, ladies."

"*Morgen*, Frank," Amanda chirped as she headed for the kitchen.

"Mornin', Frank, it's *gut* to see you." Mary dished out a smile.

He chuckled. "Never thought I'd see the Sweet Delights ladies over here in enemy territory."

Mary huffed. "Noah and I are not enemies, Frank."

"Not the way it sounds on Twitter. Sounds like a big feud. Someone took a video of you and Noah having a few heated words and posted it."

"Frank," Mary gasped. "That was just a misunderstanding."

"The newspaper has an article in it that

claims it's a feud and that's gone viral. Since there's so much commotion, the town is offering $20,000 in contest prize money instead of the $10,000. They said hundreds of bakers have already signed up for the contest."

"That's crazy. There must be some mistake." Mary propped a hip against the counter to keep her steady.

"Read the article. Over at Lazy Susan's this morning, Abigail Riggs said that you two have caused such a stir it's turned into big business for the town and the fall festival. Susan claims tourists have come to town and asked her to point you two out."

"What? Tell her not to do that."

He laughed. "If they want to pay me, I'm going to make a buck and point you out."

"You wouldn't!"

"Nah, I'm just kidding."

"Frank, are you sure about the prize money being raised to $20,000?"

"Yep. Just black coffee and a cinnamon roll, please."

Mary handed it to Frank. "On the *haus* for updating me on the news."

"Thank you. Have a good day, Mary."

She blew out a deep sigh. *Not likely now.*

The wheels on the cart squeaked as Amanda rolled it to the bakery shelves. "Did I hear Frank correctly? Did they raise the festival prize money to $20,000?"

Mary pressed her lips together then released them. "Jah, but I'm surprised we didn't hear about it."

Noah opened the back door to the kitchen and tromped in and out, carrying in his pastries.

Mary rushed from the bakery to the kitchen. "Noah, did you hear about the festival committee raising the baking prize to $20,000?"

"Yes." He pulled a newspaper out of his back pocket and handed it to Mary.

She unfolded the paper and read a few lines. "I can't believe they did this." She shook the article as she spoke.

Noah nodded. "The rumor is they expect

maybe twenty to thirty thousand to attend the festival."

She looked up from reading. "Just because they think we're feuding?"

"Finish reading the article." He stood with his back propped against the counter, feet crossed, waiting.

"What!" Mary shrieked. "MyBaking Channel contacted the festival committee. They want to send a celebrity chef as a judge. The committee has agreed," she mumbled as she read. "MyBaking Channel is sending Simone André. She is offering the winner a chance to come to her show to make the winning dessert." She stopped reading and glanced at Noah.

He nodded. "The stakes just got higher, Mary. Winner takes all."

Jenny slipped into the kitchen, poured a cup of coffee and sat at the table. "So MyBaking Channel is going to judge? That will really bring in the contestants. You two better have great recipes."

Noah shot his sister a frown. "Nice to

see you have confidence in me, sis. Sorry, I have to finish unloading." He banged the door on his way outside.

Jenny turned to Mary. "You know I didn't mean that. You both are great bakers and either of you could win."

"I know." Mary poured a cup of coffee, sat on the stool by Jenny and sipped the brew. "This is unbelievable, all because we had a fight on TV."

"It's crazy but wonderful." Jenny stood. "Stop by my office before you go home, I want to show you a web page I made for Sweet Delights. It's my way of saying thanks for all the sweets you feed me." She added as she headed out the swinging door. "Practice hard, Mary."

Amanda caught the door and carried in empty pastry pans from the bakery. "I heard Jenny's comment, but Noah is one terrific baker."

"*Jah*, he's *gut*. Now with the prize money so high, and MyBaking Channel sending Simone André as a judge, and she's offering the winner a chance to bake their winning dish on her show, the bakers will come from all over the country to enter the contest." Mary squeezed her eyes closed. *Dear Lord, You've taken away my bakery, now with the stakes so high, culinary-trained bakers will enter the contest, and I won't have a chance to win. Lord, please strengthen my ability.*

After lunch, Mary stopped in to Jenny's office just as Ethan was leaving. "Sorry, I didn't mean to disturb you." Ethan gave them a wave as he walked out.

"It's fine. He was just leaving. We're just friends, but I told him I was going to nursing school. I wasn't sure if he was getting serious or not, but he was okay with it. He knew I wasn't going to join the Order." She touched a key on her computer. "So here is your web page."

Mary gasped. "It's *wunderbaar. Danki*, that is lovely." She gave Jenny a hug. "I see you have boxed up your things. I'm going to miss you when you go."

"I'll miss you, too, but I'll be home for visits."

Mary dried a tear as she headed back to the kitchen. She started the bread dough for the next day and set it in the refrigerator to rise.

At 4:00 p.m., Noah rushed into the kitchen with worry lining his forehead. He glanced at the clock, then at Mary. "Emily is late coming home from school. Have you seen her?"

"*Nein*, not today, but the other day she told me she was spending a lot of time with a new friend. Maybe she's at her *haus*."

"She's supposed to tell me when she's going to Kate's."

The back door swung open, and Emily ran into the kitchen.

"Where have you been, young lady?" Noah hunched down to look in her face. "You're to tell me when you go to your friend's house."

"I know, but I wasn't at Kate's house. I was petting King. He was neighing and prancing around the corral. He wants to go for a walk."

"Please don't go into the corral without Mary's or my permission," Noah warned.

"Can Mary take me for a ride?" Emily wiggled around. "Please, Noah?"

"Mary is busy."

Emily ran to Mary, threw her arms around her waist and gave her a hug. "Please, Mary?"

Mary laughed and patted Emily's back. "Tell you what, when I'm ready to go home at five, I'll give you a ride."

"Great!" Emily giggled. "I'll take my stuff to my room and be back."

When Mary finished her prep work for the next day, Emily timed it just right and breezed through the swinging door. She grabbed her bag. "Are you ready for the ride?"

"Mary, would it be all right if Noah came with us?" Emily asked.

Noah entered the kitchen. "Where are we going?"

"For a buggy ride. I want you to come with us, Noah. Please?"

Noah glanced at Mary.

"Sure, if he wants to tag along, that would be fine."

Noah nodded toward the door. "Why don't you two go ahead? I'll finish here and lock up."

Mary led Emily outside to the corral and demonstrated how to hitch King to the buggy, letting her help at times. The procedure took twice as long as normal, but it was worth it. "Well done, Emily,"

Her little face glowed with the accomplishment. Emily ran around, jumped in the buggy and grabbed the reins. "Can I drive King?"

"I'll let you drive up to the door so we can pick up Noah, and we'll see how you do."

Noah was waiting. He raised his brow at Mary as he stepped in and sat on the seat next to her.

She gulped as he settled back. Her heart beat so hard she was scared he could hear the racket. She drew a steadying breath. "Emily wanted to drive, so I said we'd give it a try." She leaned back, but her arm touched his, sending a tidal wave of emotions through her. *Jah*, this might not have been such a *gut* idea.

Mary tugged the reins to the right. "Let's turn down Fifth Street, go past the fire station and turn right onto J Avenue."

Emily pushed Mary's hand away. "I can do it by myself."

King jerked the buggy into motion and picked up speed. Mary raised her hand and leaned toward Emily. "Slow King down, Emily"

"I don't know how to do that. He's going so fast."

"*Jah*, I will help you. When he's been corralled all day, he gets antsy and wants to stretch his legs." Mary laid her hand over Emily's and gently showed her how to pull back on the reins. "Do you feel what I'm doing? Tugging back tells him to go slower. When you want to turn right, tug the reins right, and he knows to turn right. The same with left."

Emily heaved a long sigh. "Oh, that's easy."

Mary could feel Emily relax back into the seat. If only she could do the same, but with Noah so close, that was impossible. His nearness was suffocating her. Moisture dampened her palms. "How do you like the buggy ride, Noah?"

"The seat is much more comfortable than I thought it would be, and the ride is fun."

As King turned onto J Avenue, the buggy wheel hit a rut in the road and bounced. Noah swayed and brushed against Mary. He recovered quickly and straightened. He was so close she could hear him breathing. Pressing a hand over her heart, she tried to calm it. She had to quit thinking about him. "So Noah, do you have your recipes picked for the contest?"

"I do, but I'll practice them a few more times to make sure they're perfect. How about you?"

"*Jah*, I was debating between two apple pie recipes, but I've made the selection. Having to bake three days in a row for the three-day contest is stressful." Mary leaned toward Emily. "Turn right onto Fourteenth Street."

Emily pulled back on the reins as they approached the turn then tugged the reins right. King turned the corner smoothly. Emily laughed. "I did it."

Mary reached an arm around her and squeezed. "You are really getting the hang of it. You're a natural."

The clip-clopping of King's hooves were soothing and Mary even started to enjoy Noah sitting beside her. "Slow King down, Emily, and turn onto A Avenue."

"He won't slow down." Emily worried her bottom lip.

"Do you want me to help you? Sometimes King has a mind of his own."

"Yes, I'm scared."

Mary put her hand on the reins and firmly pulled back. "King, settle down." Her voice had a sharp ring. The horse wanted to get out on the road and go, but he'd just have to wait a while longer.

Settling back in the seat, she brushed against Noah and the touch sent her heart racing again. What was wrong with her? She was acting like a silly schoolgirl. "Turn onto Fifth Street when you come to it."

"Okay."

Another buggy approached them from the opposite direction. Mary poised her hand midair in case Emily got nervous, and she needed to grab the reins. The buggy neared, and Mary's heart dropped. "Oh, no."

"Something wrong?" Noah sounded concerned.

"I'm fine. I didn't mean to say that." She could sense Noah staring at her. "Sometimes King can get a little skittish when another horse is near."

But that wasn't it. As the other buggy drew alongside, she turned and saw Bishop Yoder's warning stare aimed in her direction. The bishop had counseled her about

Noah once before. No doubt he would be paying her a visit after seeing her snuggled up next to Noah Miller in a buggy.

Now, she'd be confessing her sin for sure and for certain.

Chapter Fourteen

When Noah stopped his vehicle and parked in his grandpa's drive, Cyrus hurried out of the toolshed and headed his way wearing a scowl.

He stopped six-feet away. "Look, Noah, it's great that you come out to visit *Daed* and help him on the farm, but it's sending mixed signals. My parents have hopes that you're going to join our community." Cyrus's tone changed from impatient to one of concern. "I think we both know you're not going to do that. *Daed* is in the milking room, disinfecting the floor and stanchions.

But it would be best if you left and didn't come out again."

The words bombarded Noah one after the other. He silently nodded and climbed back in the SUV, a knot twisting in his stomach. His hands gripped the steering wheel while his heart plummeted to his feet. He understood his uncle's concern, but that didn't make the situation easier.

Where the gravel road met the highway, Noah turned toward Iowa City. He couldn't face Mary just yet. She'd ask him how it went at his grandpa's farm, and he didn't want to talk about it.

He parked behind his store and tried to muster up a friendly smile. His keys jangled as he unlocked the back door and stepped into a warm kitchen smelling of cinnamon and yeast rolls.

Sidney looked up. "Hi, boss. Since it's Friday morning, I didn't expect to see you today."

"How about some help? I need to do some

thinking, and the kitchen is where I do it best."

"Always glad for the help." Sidney gave him a curious glance but went back to his work.

When he left later that day, Noah called Jenny and let her know he was heading to their grandparents' farm for a short bit before heading home. He parked in their drive, hoping Cyrus had gone home. He climbed the porch and knocked on the kitchen door.

Soft footfalls approached just before Grandma pushed the screen open. "Come in."

When Noah entered, his grandpa was sitting at the oak kitchen, eating supper. His grandma took her chair.

"Sorry to bother you," Noah said.

"Sit," Grandpa invited. "Are you hungry?"

"No, thanks. I'm only going to stay a minute." Noah rubbed his palms across the pockets of his trousers. For as long as he could remember, he had wanted to meet his grandparents and get to know them. But he had to do what was fair for everyone.

His grandmother was quiet, and he could see her uneasy gaze dart from his grandpa to Noah. His plan before he left Iowa City sounded good. Now, he wasn't so sure.

"Grandpa, Cyrus said he thinks it's best if I don't hang around here. I was wondering if that's the way you feel, too?"

The old man stopped eating and laid his fork on his plate. "Most times, Cyrus and I don't see eye to eye, but this time, he's right. The bishop doesn't like a lot of fraternizing with the *Englisch*. It can give the youngies the wrong idea."

Grandma sat with her head down, slowly eating. She didn't acknowledge the conversation.

"Okay. I'm sorry it has to be this way, but I understand. I enjoyed getting to know you both." The words caught in Noah's throat and stumbled out.

Silence stretched across the room.

Noah turned and walked out of the house,

quietly closing the door between him and his grandparents.

The goodbye cut deep into his heart. He wanted to be part of their family. But he couldn't give up his SUV for a horse and buggy, he needed his vehicle. He owned an expanding business, and he had responsibilities. But that didn't make the knot in his stomach go away.

The way he was shut out of his grandparents' world, he would probably soon be shut out of Mary's life, too.

Lord, God, I don't know where You're leading me, but I pray it's for the betterment of my family. Because it's tearing my heart in two.

When she heard the grocery door open, Mary had a feeling it was Bishop Yoder. She slowly lifted her gaze from her work at the bakery counter to the visitor, and blew out a long breath. "*Gut Morgen,* Ethan. I'm glad it's you."

"That's the best thing I've heard all day.

It's nice to see you, too." Ethan livened his step to the counter. "Why are you glad to see me?" He removed his straw hat and rubbed it across his blue chambray shirt and suspenders.

"When I heard the door, I thought it was the bishop. Emily wanted to go for a buggy ride yesterday. I let her have the reins, and I sat next to Noah. The bishop saw us and gave me a warning look."

"Ah, the *warning look*. I know it well from my early *rumspringa* days. Tell the bishop you were bringing Noah out to see me."

"Shame on you, I couldn't lie. Besides, it was a harmless buggy ride. So what would you like today?"

"A double-chocolate donut and a black coffee."

She set his order on the counter. Ethan handed her the money, picked up his purchase, and turned to go but stopped.

Mary's eyes followed his stare.

Bishop Yoder held the door while Bishop Ropp entered.

Mary cringed. How long had they been standing there?

Ethan hurried out the door while Bishop Ropp walked around the bakery section, trying to decide what he wanted.

Bishop Yoder's stare was icy as he approached the counter. "Mary," he whispered, "you are making a mistake running around with that *Englischer.*"

She clenched her fist. "I'm not involved with Noah. He generously offered me space in his store so I can keep customers with standing orders."

"It's time you thought about getting married, *jah*?"

She cringed. "Did you forget that just a year ago Seth dumped me to go live with the *Englisch*? And after we both had been baptized and joined the church."

"I haven't forgotten, but our faith tells us to forgive. Seth was immature. He was not ready to settle down when he decided to get married. He has repented and went through and the rite of restoration. He's back now and willing to pick up where you two left off."

Mary straightened her back and sucked in a deep breath. "I can't believe you're encouraging me to marry him."

"He cares for you in spite of his careless actions. Think about it rationally, you will see he's a *gut* fit for you."

"Mary," Bishop Ropp interrupted. "Do you have any Bismarcks with the lemon filling like Sarah's papa's partner often made?"

"No... Sarah never mentioned her vater had a partner. Who was he?"

"That's too many years ago, I can't remember his name." He waved a hand in the air as if to bat the question away.

Mary stared at the old bishop, hoping he wasn't getting senile. "Do either of you wish to make a purchase?"

They each shook their heads.

The old bishop shuffled out the door as Bishop Yoder held it open. As he turned to leave, he tossed Mary a stern look. "Go for a buggy ride, Mary, and give Seth a chance to explain. You know as well as I do that Noah will never give up his *Englisch* ways. If you leave our church, you will be shunned." When the bishop let go, the door banged shut.

She'd never marry Seth Knepp, no matter what the bishop said. But he was right about one thing, Noah would never give up the *Englisch* ways.

The swinging door from the kitchen creaked and Noah's footfalls grew louder with each approaching step.

She turned as he reached the counter. His brow was creased, and lines pulled at his eyes. "You look tired. Did you do a lot of work helping your *grossdaddi*?"

Noah stood silent a moment. "I drove out to help grandpa. Cyrus met me in the drive and said he thought it would be better if I didn't come out there anymore. He claimed my grandparents were getting their hopes up that I'd join the community, which I have no intention of doing. I drove back out to see them when Cyrus was gone, and my grandpa said the same thing."

Mary flinched at his admission that he wasn't going to join their community. "Noah, I'm so sorry they feel that way. But our bishop doesn't encourage friendships with the *Englisch*."

"I understand, but I was still hoping for some kind of relationship." He turned and headed back to the kitchen. "Have a good evening, Mary."

Jah, she knew that wasn't what Noah wanted to hear. The bishop paying her a visit today was a not-so-subtle hint to her, too, about the same thing.

Mary grabbed a wet cloth and started to tidy up the bakery counter before she left for home. She turned at the sound of shoes tapping the flooring toward the counter. "Jenny, I haven't seen you all day. You must be really busy."

"I'm glad you haven't left yet, Mary. I'm in the process of packing, and I'll leave for school this weekend. I wanted to make sure I said goodbye."

After blotting tears from her eyes, Mary crushed Jenny in a hug. Over her days here at the store, she and Jenny spent many coffee breaks together each day talking about their girlhood, growing up and their dreams. "I'll miss you and will pray for your success on the journey that *Gott* has set your feet upon."

"Thank you. I appreciate that." Jenny stepped back with tears escaping down her cheek. She dug in her pocket, pulled out a tissue and wiped them away.

Mary swallowed hard. Her life had changed so much in just a few short weeks. She loved her *Englisch* friends and didn't want to say goodbye to Jenny…or to Noah.

Chapter Fifteen

Saturday, Mary laid a dozen strips of bacon in the iron skillet and fried a dozen eggs in another. She pulled the hot biscuits from the oven and scooped them into a waiting breadbasket with a small towel laid in the bottom.

She flipped the bacon then turned the eggs. Hurrying to the gas refrigerator, Mary pulled out the milk, orange juice, and butter and set them in the middle of the table.

The kitchen screen door squeaked as *Daed* stepped in from the porch, crossed the kitchen and set a bucket of milk on the counter next to her. "Morgen, Mary."

"Gut Morgen, Daed."

"Are you running late getting to the store?"

"Nein, Amanda is starting our bread and rolls this morning. I wanted to help *Mamm* since the twins have a cold."

Daed cleared his throat. "I ran into Bishop Yoder yesterday in town."

Mary recognized that tone from when she'd misbehaved as a young girl. She squared her shoulders for the lecture that no doubt would follow.

"He said you were out riding in the buggy with Noah Miller." His words held an edge. "You know he's not the kind of man you should be seeing. His values are different than yours."

"We're not involved in a personal relationship. I work in his store. Emily badgered me for a buggy ride, and she wanted Noah to ride along. I couldn't very well say no. I'm not going to treat him rudely."

"I wouldn't expect you to, but he is a nice-looking lad, and I wouldn't want you to get your expectations up and your feelings hurt. From what I've heard, he's not planning on joining our community."

"*Daed*, the bishop insinuated that since Seth is back, I should consider allowing him to court me again. Did he mention that to you?"

"It would be understandable for the bishop to think that. At one time, you had your heart set on marrying him."

She drew a deep breath, simmered down and blew it out. "I'm not leaving my faith, and I'm not going to marry Seth. That's over and done with."

"Listen, *tochter*, I do worry, as every Amish *vater* does that one day his *kinner* might want to try the world of the *Englisch*. I've seen the hurt on many parents' faces."

She nodded. "I know. I felt it when Seth left, and that's why I could never trust him again. And it's why I could never trust Noah Miller."

Daed patted her shoulder. "*Jah, liebe* hurts sometimes. I have a surprise for you. The

Plain community plans to start rebuilding Sweet Delights next Monday, so it should be ready in no time. Of course, it will only have the basics inside. Since the fire started in the old wiring, there might have been an overload so I asked for more electrical outlets and an additional circuit breaker. That will make it safer."

"That's *wunderbaar.*" Mary lunged at her *daed* and threw her arms around him. *"Danki."*

Jacob and Michael Paul tore through the door from the porch, washed up and raced to the table for breakfast.

"I beat you." The four-year-old beamed.

"You are the best at running, munchkin." Jacob nodded.

Mary dished up breakfast and walked to the doorway. *"Mamm,* breakfast is ready."

Sarah slid onto the chair next to Mary and gave her a hug. *"Danki,* sweetheart."

After cleaning the kitchen, Mary headed her buggy to town.

As she entered the kitchen, Noah glanced her way. "Morning."

"*Jah*, you're back from the other store already?"

"I didn't go to Iowa City this morning. I wanted to practice my entries. I heard the festival committee has received a thousand entries. They're going to eliminate most in the first round with three rounds of judging. That means our entries will need to be perfect."

"Where did you hear that?"

"They sent out letters. Your mail is lying on the counter over there." He gestured toward the end of the counter.

"*Danki.* With that many entries, I'll never win."

"Don't sell yourself short, Mary. You're a wonderful baker."

After reading her mail, she pulled out her ingredients, stirred up chocolate chip cookies and began dropping them on a cookie sheet with two spoons.

Noah grabbed two spoons, stood beside Mary, and began to help.

"Danki."

"Don't mention it." His hand bumped hers as they both went for the same spot of dough. His touch sent a tingle up her arm. She inhaled a controlling breath and blew it out slowly, trying to hide the thumping in her chest. "Hey, Noah, I'm planning on winning the contest, just so you know."

He laughed. "That's funny, because I plan on winning it."

"Jah, and so does every one of those bakers that entered."

He dropped several cookies on the sheet. "Mary, tell me about your faith."

"We live by Romans 12:12, 'be not conformed to this world.' We seek to lose the idea of self and live instead for the community and putting others first. We believe happiness comes from putting Jesus first, others next and ourselves last."

Noah stopped his hands a second and

glanced her way. "Would it be possible for me to visit your church sometime?"

Her heart skipped a beat. She finished dropping the last cookie, set her spoons down and popped the sheet in the oven. "Church Sunday is tomorrow, and it's your grandparents' turn to host. That might be a *gut* time for you to visit. It's a three-hour service, then a common meal at noon." A few minutes later, she pulled the cookies from the oven.

She glanced at Noah and tried to read his face. Was he thinking about joining the Old Order or just curious? But she wouldn't allow this to give her false hope.

Noah gathered the baking pans and set them in the sink. "How about we practice our entries again? I could help you if you need an extra pair of hands."

Mary tossed him a wry smile. "Oh no, you don't, you're not tasting it."

Laughing, he scooped a big bag of apples from the cooler. "You don't trust me?"

She pulled a bowl and colander from a cupboard and faced him. "Based on my experience with Seth, trust is more fragile than *liebe*."

"Someday, Mary, I hope you find someone you can love and trust." When he reached for an apple, her hand was already there, and his slipped over her soft skin. His heart galloped at her nearness as his fingers fumbled to grasp an apple. He wanted to reach over and pull her into his embrace, press a kiss to her lips and never let her go. He wanted to be that someone she could love and trust...but it wasn't going to happen.

She grabbed an apple and pulled her hand away quickly. He stepped to the side to calm his racing pulse, pretending to give her more room.

It was nice having Mary in his kitchen every day. He was going to miss her, miss her smile, and miss her sweetness when she went back to her bakery.

He opened the oven door, and they both set their pies on a hot rack. "How about a muffin and a glass of tea?" His gaze caught hers and held it for a second.

"*Jah*, a break sounds *gut* right about now." She followed him to the baked goods in the front of the store.

He handed her a poppy seed muffin. "Try this and tell me what you think." He poured two glasses of tea while she ate. "Has your dad decided yet whether to rebuild Sweet Delights?"

"*Jah*, just this *morgen* he said our community is going to raise it a week from Monday. But the new structure will only have the bare minimum in it. I still need to win in order to buy the extra things I need to expand the menu. So next Monday, I'll stay busy baking for the workers."

"That's not a problem. I can watch Sweet Delights while you and Amanda bake for the workers."

"Noah, why the interest in our church?" She took another bite of muffin. "Mmm."

He shrugged. "I just want more information about the Amish faith so I can understand my grandparents and their ways better." He bit into his muffin.

Mary licked a crumb from her lip. "Where did you get this poppy seed recipe? It's divine."

"From Mom's collection. My recipes are from either Mom or Dad. My great-grandfather owned a bakery until he died, and my father helped him. That's how Dad got interested in starting his own bakery which he then expanded into the farm-fresh grocery and delicatessen."

Mary turned quiet. Noah glanced at her, and followed her gaze until he saw Bishop Yoder's frowning face and Seth standing next to him.

"So here you are, Mary." Seth said as if he had a right to know her whereabouts.

Noah flinched as if he'd been caught smoking behind the barn.

"What do you want, Seth?" Mary's voice whipped across the aisle at her ex-fiancé.

"Just to talk."

"*Nein.* I don't want to talk to you, and quit

telling people you want to pick up where we ended. Because as the word says, it's ended."

Noah felt the tension. This conversation was none of his concern. He took a step back, turned and slipped quietly away. He heard Mary's footfalls close behind as he pushed the swinging door open and held it for her. As soon as she entered, he closed it. "Are you okay?"

"*Jah.* Seth's been telling the bishop and *Daed*, I think, that he wants to court me again, hoping the bishop will talk me into it. But I can't trust him, and I'm not going back with him. Ever. Seth doesn't know if he wants to live as *Englisch* or Amish. He's an Englischer, and that's what we call an *Auswendiger*—an outsider. He can't be trusted!"

Noah took a step back. Mary's words stabbed at his gut. She didn't trust *Englischers*.

Chapter Sixteen

On Sunday morning, Noah parked in his grandparents' barnyard at the end of a long line of buggies. He glanced at the cloudy sky, hoping the rain would hold off, then ran his hands over his suit coat to smooth any wrinkles and prayed his attire was appropriate.

He walked to the barn and stopped inside the doorway. The women sat on one side and men on the other. His gaze scanned the benches until it caught Mary's eye. She tilted her head toward the men. He skirted around the benches and found a spot on the last one…next to Mary's ex-fiancé, his cousin. Seth nodded, and Noah sat.

The bench was hard, and Noah sensed the tension filling the space between him and Seth. In a few minutes, a man announced a hymn number and started the singing, which they all joined in, except the preachers, who left the area. When they returned, the singing stopped. The preachers sat, but one remained standing and spoke a few opening words.

He began, "Blessed be the God…"

He concluded with a reminder to the congregation to prepare their hearts and listen to the Word of God and to trust God. He spoke in a mixture of Pennsylvania-Dutch, German and English, which put Noah at ease for a few minutes.

After prayer, a preacher began the main sermon. "May grace and mercy be with you and the peace of *Gott*." Words Noah had often heard his mom speak in German.

Mary had prepared him, but the service seemed never ending. He tried not to squirm, but it was hard. Since his parents had spoken German, he understood a few words and phrases. The minister said a few words in English, Noah thought for his benefit: "Be ye not unequally yoked together with unbelievers."

The rest of the sermon was a blur. When it was over, Seth stood and disappeared with a crowd of men without saying a word. Noah jabbed his hands in his pockets and mulled around. It was tempting to leave, but he'd wait until after the meal. The men congregated in their own groups, so he strayed away from them. He looked around, but his grandpa was busy.

"*Hallo*, Noah. I didn't expect to see you here."

He jerked around and let out a soft sigh. "Hello, Aunt Judith. Well, I was curious."

"Are you thinking about joining our Order? That would be *wunderbaar*."

"After meeting the family, I wanted to understand your religion and what you believe." Guilt squeezed his chest. Truth was, his parents' death had torn his heart in two, and he was tired of hurting and feeling alone. He was angry at God for the accident that killed them, and it was time he got right with Him. He wanted to find God, have it out with Him, and make Him say why He had to take them. And he figured he'd find God at their church.

"*Danki* for coming, Noah," Judith said. "Whether our *daed* says it or not, I know he enjoyed seeing you here."

"I haven't talked to him. I'm not sure he knows I'm here."

"He knows you're here. I saw him watching you. Maybe I'll see you later. But now I must help serve the meal."

Noah turned and almost ran into Mary. "I was wondering if I'd see you."

"I'm helping the women, but I thought I'd better tell you that the men all eat together at that long table." She pointed, and he nodded.

The men didn't ask his name. But he was sure they recognized him as Thomas Miller's grandson, from his *Englisch* son Jeremiah. But no one acted like they were curious enough to ask what he was doing here. Or they were just polite.

Noah ate his meal with the men on either side of him asking him casual questions. It helped ease the butterflies churning in his gut.

When he saw Mary cleaning up after the meal, he excused himself and headed in her direction.

He sprinted the last few yards. "Hello, Mary."

She turned toward him. "What did you think?"

"It was nice, different. Sometimes I thought the preachers were talking directly to me."

She smiled. "They were talking to all of us."

"Emily stayed with a friend, and I said I'd pick her up on the way home. So I need to get going, but I'll see you tomorrow at work." He glanced past her, and noticed that her dad had a bead on him. She'd been hurt once before, and judging by Caleb's face, he wasn't going to let his daughter get hurt again. "Is my grandma in the house?" Noah asked. "I want to say goodbye to her."

"*Jah*, I'm sure she'd be upset if you didn't."

He stepped inside the kitchen and spotted his grandmother at the sink. "I need to get going," he said, "but I wanted to say goodbye."

She walked out onto the porch with him. "*Danki* for coming, and I'm sure Thomas is glad, too. No matter what Cyrus said to you, I want you to come back and visit."

Noah enveloped her in a hug and then kissed her cheek. "I'll be back to visit sometime."

Her smiled reached all the way to her eyes. She turned and headed back to the kitchen.

Noah swallowed hard and wandered across the yard to his vehicle, blinking a tear from his eye. He rubbed a hand across the aching in his chest. He loved them already...and he was going to miss them.

For a week, Mary baked for the tourists and practiced her three entries required for the three days of baking for the contest.

Monday morning, she grabbed the pot-holders, pulled two loaves of bread out of the oven and set them on the cooling racks. Standing back, she watched Amanda fill a jellyroll pan with cinnamon rolls and pop them in the oven.

"Amanda, I'm going to take this cart of honey-wheat and white bread to the front so it'll be ready to run across the street later for the men working at Sweet Delights."

"I'm right behind carrying cupcakes and sugar cookies." Amanda exchanged the pot-holders for a tray and fell into step behind her.

Mary parked the cart in the front of the store, the door opened and Jean whirled in and quickly closed the door before a gust of wind could blow a pile of rustling leaves inside. "Good morning, ladies. It's nippy out today."

"Mornin', Jean. Fall is just around the corner." Mary backed the cart farther away from the entrance.

The door flew open again, and Ethan Lapp scrambled in. "*Morgen*, Mary. Amanda."

"You, too." Amanda said as she started to arrange the sugar cookies and cupcakes on a shelf. Mary looked up. "Morgen, Ethan. You're not working at the bakery raising?"

"*Jah*, I just stopped in to say hi."

His eyes strayed from her. "How are you, Amanda?"

"*Jah*, I'm *gut*." She kept on working.

Mary had the feeling that maybe Ethan and Amanda wanted to talk. "Ethan, when you go back, will you roll this cart of bread and rolls over to *Mamm* so she can set them out for lunch for the workers?" Without waiting for his reply, she picked up the empty pans and carried them back to the kitchen.

She tidied up the counter and washed the sink full of dishes. Twenty minutes later, Amanda walked in.

"So what was that all about with Ethan?" Curiosity pulled the words out of Mary.

Amanda pulled a bowl from the cupboard,

clunked it on the counter and started to make a cake. "Nothing really. Ethan's just started coming around and talking."

"Are you two a couple?" Mary whispered.

"Nein." Amanda paused. "I'm not sure what we're doing. It seems we're just talking." A little smile tugged at the corners of her mouth. "He might have said more, but he needed to get back to work. Where's Noah?"

"He left a note saying he was taking jugs of tea and coffee to Sweet Delights for the workers. Are you purposely trying to get off the subject of Ethan?"

"Okay, the other day he stopped by, and we just started talking about the festival and things."

"So has he asked you to go on a buggy ride?"

"Nein, we're just friends."

Why was it that neither she nor Amanda had snagged their perfect love? Why was it that both of them wanted what they couldn't have?

Mary sighed. It was harder each day seeing Noah knowing he was *Englisch* and that nothing was going to happen between them.

He would glance at her when he thought she wasn't watching, and she'd felt the spark when their hands accidently touched. She'd frozen in place and couldn't breathe. Now, she could still feel the tingle on her hand… and in her heart. But that was as far as it could go.

Opening the back door of the store, Noah dashed through and laid Mary's mail beside her. "We have our schedule from the festival contest director."

Mary whirled around to face him. "Have you read yours?"

He nodded. "We have to take our first entry to the judge next Thursday for the first-round judging. They will eliminate all but three in each of the three categories. On Friday, those nine will bake, and they'll pick a winner in each of the three categories. The winners will receive $5,000. On Saturday, those three winners compete for the trophy and grand prize of $20,000."

"You're a world of news." Mary tore open her contest letter and read.

"I hope you're ready, Mary."

She smiled and her eyes locked with his. "Game on, Noah."

Her voice was soft and melted into him like butter. "Ready to get busy and practice?"

She jerked her gaze from his. "Jah, let's get busy."

Noah pulled out the canister of flour, and they each practiced their entry one more time. He watched Mary slide hers in the oven on the bottom rack, and he set his on the top rack and closed the door.

Emily burst in through the back door and ran to Noah. "Can I compete in the children's baking contest at the festival?" she begged. "They're still taking entries. One of the prizes is a pink backpack."

He shrugged. "Sure. You're a good baker. Mary saw to that." He glanced at Mary and detected a hint of a smile cross her face before it discretely disappeared. "Do you know what you want to make?"

"Yes, peanut butter bars. I can win, Noah, my recipe is really, really good. My friend Kate is going to enter, too."

Mary handed a measuring cup to Emily. "Do you want to make a practice one now, and I'll watch?"

"Sure." Emily gathered her ingredients and carefully measured each one out.

Noah took a step back and leaned against the sink. Emily liked Mary, and for that matter, so did he. Maybe too much.

Mary lifted her cornflower-blue eyes and locked them with his. His chest thumped like he was a schoolboy with a crush.

He grabbed a tray of bread and headed to the front of the store. What was he doing? Where could this relationship go? He was *Englisch*, she was Amish, and neither was willing to change.

Chapter Seventeen

On Wednesday, Mary pulled out a tablet and pencil and sat at the table in the store's kitchen. She wrote a schedule for herself and a baking schedule for Amanda. The next week would be hectic with extra baking for the tourists and festivalgoers, and creating perfect entries for the contest.

Noah rushed into the kitchen from the back door and threw open the pantry doors. He pulled out his pocket notebook and pen and jotted down things as he mumbled to himself. "We're running low on baking powder and flour. I'm going to run to Iowa City and get extra supplies. I spoke to Susan on the street and told her I'd pick up some supplies for her restaurant, too. Is there anything you can think of that we need?"

"More sugar," Mary answered without looking up from her list. She tried to ignore the tingling in her stomach whenever he was around. She kept her gaze down and made another note.

"Would you like to ride over to my store in Iowa City while I pick up a few things? You've never seen it, and it's only eighteen miles. Shouldn't take too long."

She raised her head. "*Jah*, I'd like to see your other store."

Thirty minutes later, Noah pulled up to the front of his store in Iowa City. "I'll let you out here. You can walk through, and I'll meet you at the back door."

She stepped out of his vehicle, shocked to see that this store was twice the size of the one in Kalona. She gravitated to the bakery section first. He had a few desserts and pastries here that weren't at the other one. They looked delicious. Now she was curious about how the rest of this store would be different.

He had an elegant coffee stand with a beautiful cappuccino and latte maker. A full salad bar was in the middle of the deli section with fresh vegetables and fruits. There were not only cold sandwiches, but a woman behind a counter was making grilled cheese, hamburgers, paninis and pizzas.

In Kalona, she had thought of Noah as a shop owner, but his talents spanned much more than just a small shop. She walked through the large produce area. He had all this to take care of and he still helped his grandparents. And he was giving her a hand, as well.

She weaved her way through the kitchen to the service door at the back and found Noah loading his SUV.

"What do you think?" A hint of pride was visible in his expression.

"It's bigger than I imagined. Your bakery here has a larger selection of pastries. It appears you learned the trade of your *vater* very well."

His smiled stretched all the way to his amber eyes, and his five o'clock stubble gave him a rugged but handsome look. He motioned to his vehicle parked at the open door. "Ready to go back to Kalona?"

"*Jah*, I need to get my baking done. I don't have a fancy store like this to support me." She teased as she climbed in and fastened the seatbelt.

He buckled up and started the engine. "I'm saving every dime I get out of this store to pay for Emily's college, and Jenny's, if she'll let me pay. But Jenny said she didn't want to work in the store, so she didn't want to take money from the business. But it's hers, too."

"Jenny owns a portion of the business? In the Plain community, it would have gone to the son."

"When our parents died, I put everything they owned in all three of our names. So if anything happens to me, they'd have a means to pay for their schooling or a way to support themselves. But as you probably know, the Amish in Kalona weren't coming to my store until after I gave out samples at the barn raising. Most of them patronize your bakery, Mary, and they grow their own vegetables. And as you say, Kalona is a small town, so I'm not sure I can keep that store open unless I win the contest." He glanced across the console. "You do realize whoever wins will be written up in the newspaper and in the tourist brochure. That should boost sales."

Mary's back straightened against the seat. "I'm sorry. I didn't realize that about your business. I suppose more of the Plain come to my bakery, but you have a *gut* deli business, and your pastries taste *wunderbaar*."

"Mary, my parents had said they left their community during their *rumspringa*, but I was shocked when Cyrus said my grandpa lay on the ground for hours while my dad fiddled around in town buying a bundle of shingles, which should have only taken a few minutes. That must have been why Dad pushed Jenny and me so hard."

Mary turned her head so fast her *kapp* strings swung back and forth. "*Nein*, don't blame your *daed*. He was young and didn't know your *grossdaddi* had fallen. The older man shouldn't have been on the roof by himself."

"I know, but I can't get that out of my head." Noah's voice choked on the words.

Mary cleared the lump clogging her throat. She'd blamed Noah for trying to ruin her business. Now she knew that wasn't true.

The remainder of the trip was quiet as she watched the farmers in the field. Back in Kalona, Noah parked behind his store and picked up the heavy box from the SUV while Mary lifted the lighter one. She followed him in and set her carton on a shelf in the pantry.

Noah plunked his box on the floor in the back. "I have to take a couple of boxes down to Susan. Want to come along and carry one for me?"

"Sure. It shouldn't take but a few minutes to walk to Susan's restaurant."

Noah held Lazy Susan's front door open as Mary carried her box inside. She slowed her pace, and waited for Noah when Susan waved them over to the checkout counter.

As Noah's six-foot, bigger-than-life presence strolled next to her, Mary tried to keep some space between them. She looked around to see if anyone had paid attention to them walking in together. *Nein*, it didn't appear so. Everyone seemed to be talking or eating.

Was she leading Noah on by riding with him to Iowa City? There was an attraction between them, that was for sure and certain. But she could never leave her community. And Noah had made it clear he didn't intend to join their Order.

Was this just two friends working together or something else entirely? Something that shouldn't be...nein, that couldn't be.

But her heart said *something* she didn't want to hear.

* * *

Noah glanced at Mary, but she seemed deep in thought. Maybe she was worried about the contest. He stepped up to the checkout counter with his box of supplies. "Hi, Susan, where would you like these boxes?"

"Thank you, Noah, Mary," Susan greeted them with a smile. "Just set them here on the counter, and I'll have someone from the kitchen come and get them."

Noah handed her the bill. Susan took it and waved her hand toward a table. "Why don't you two take a seat? Order a sandwich and a piece of pie on the house while I write you a check." She hurried from behind the counter and headed toward the office.

Noah gestured at a booth. "How about lunch?"

Mary glanced at the front door then back at him. "I'll just have a piece of pie. I have things to do and need to get back to the store." She slid into the closest booth, and Noah sat opposite her.

After the server set their water down and scooted away with their order, Noah leaned back and blew out a sigh. "It's nice to sit and relax. You're quiet, Mary."

She ran her hand along the edge of the placemat. "Just have a lot on my mind. Making a recipe that'll beat yours for the contest, and Sweet Delights is almost ready to open." She kept her gaze lowered as she picked up her water glass and wiped the condensation off the bottom.

The server set their pie down and hurried away.

Somehow, he got the feeling Mary wasn't telling him something. Was it just her baking she needed to get back to? He took a sip of water, but tension hung in the air between them like smoke rising off a bonfire.

"Noah, I need to be honest with you. I'm baptized and have joined our church. That means that my actions, if deemed inappropriate by the *Gmay*, could be disciplined. The bishop has warned me about spending too much time with you."

He jerked and sloshed water from the glass he was holding. He set it on the coaster and flopped back against the seat. "Mary, I'm sorry. I didn't realize it was such a problem, but we work together. This is only a temporary situation."

He never should have asked her to come to such a public place with him. It wasn't fair to put her in an awkward situation. What was he thinking? They were from different worlds. It was an impossible situation for both of them.

You're a fool, Miller. Let her go.

Mary took a bite of pie, looked up and into the stare of Bishop Yoder approaching her table. Her fork dropped to her plate, and a piece of crust flopped onto the table.

The bishop approached and stood by her side. "Mary, could I have a few words with you?" His voice was low, but others at tables nearby looked their way.

Noah glanced at Mary. "I need to get back to the store. I'll excuse myself, and you can sit in my place, Bishop." He slid off the seat and headed toward Susan at checkout.

Bishop Yoder sat opposite Mary, taking Noah's seat. He pushed Noah's dishes off to the side and laid his clasped hands on the table in front of him. His face was solemn. "Mary, you have been baptized and joined the church. That means you have chosen to submit to the *Ordnung* and the *Gmay*."

Mary gulped a ragged breath. "Bishop, I know, but I have done nothing wrong."

He shook his head. "Do not allow this *Englischer* to court you. He attended church, but other than that, he has given no indication that he wants to join our Order."

"I work with Noah. We picked up supplies for our kitchen, and Susan asked us to bring back a few things for her." Mary kept her attention on the pie, picking at it with her fork, except for a quick glance at the bishop's face.

"Listen to me, Mary." He tapped his hand softly on the edge of the table. "I think you have told yourself that. At your baptism, you promised to obey the regulations. Has that changed?"

A streak of pain tore through her and dropped to the pit of her stomach. "You're right, Bishop. I have been letting my heart overrule my head and what I have professed with my lips. I will move out of Noah's store next week. By then, Sweet Delights will be far enough along. I can work inside and get it ready to open."

The bishop stood. "*Jah*, I don't believe we will need to have this conversation again. I will let you finish your pie in peace and in prayer."

What was she thinking? She should have kept her distance from Noah.

She'd only be at his store for a few more days. Tomorrow was Thursday and the day her first contest entry was due. She and Noah were competitors once again. This time she needed to keep her focus on the prize, otherwise Noah, or someone else, would win the $20,000.

Chapter Eighteen

Thursday morning, Mary hitched King at 4:00 a.m. and headed to Noah's store.

Lord Gott, all that I do is to serve You. If I fail in any way, please lead my feet back on the right path so that my work glorifies Your name. I hope that my will is in line with Your will for me and Sweet Delights. But truly, Father, I don't know what I'd do if I lost the bakery, but Your will be done.

She reached for the doorknob and noticed the light shining through the parted curtain. Noah was already here. He thought like her, the first entry might require repeat making until they turned out perfect.

She gulped a breath and opened the door. Noah was busy at work and didn't look up, but Amanda was also in the kitchen, setting a pan of bread in the oven.

"*Danki*, Amanda, for getting here early."

Amanda tossed her a smile and winked. "I knew you would be busy all day. I'll do our baking, and you worry about getting your entry perfect."

After stowing her bag, Mary pulled eggs from the cooler and beat them until light and fluffy. She added the yeast and milk mixture, stirred and turned it out onto a floured board and began kneading the dough until it was elastic. She plopped it in a bowl, covered it and set the dough aside to rise.

She glanced over at Noah just as he raised his head from mashing bananas. He nodded and went right back to work. Strange he had said nothing to her. He was usually very talkative. Had Bishop Yoder said something to him?

Mary brushed that thought aside. She grabbed fresh strawberries, cleaned them, added sugar, a little water, and cooked the fruit down into a thick syrup. *Ach*, she forgot to add the lemon juice. She turned the fire down and hurried to the refrigerator.

A scorching aroma filled the kitchen as she slammed the fridge door closed and ran back to the stove. She jerked the pan off the burner and noticed she'd turned the flame up instead of down. Burnt!

She glanced at Noah. He didn't acknowledge the mistake. Any other time, he would have teased her. She missed his verbal quips. They broke up the day and made standing on her feet fun...because it was with him.

Grabbing another bag of strawberries, she started over. Her hand was shaking as she stirred the sauce over a low heat.

Amanda patted her on the back. "You've got this. Relax!"

When the sauce was at the right temperature and thickened, Mary removed it from the heat and set it to cool. She started the cream cheese filling and whipped it until it was light and fluffy.

She rolled out the dough into a flat rectangle, added her filling, rolled it into a log and cut the rolls into one-inch slices. When they had finished rising, Mary popped them in the oven. This had to win...it just had to.

Fifteen minutes later, she pulled the rolls from the oven and set them on a rack to cool. After a few minutes, she eased a roll off the jellyroll pan with a spatula, set it on a plate and handed it to Amanda.

Amanda took a bite and then another. "*Ach.* This is so delicious I could eat the whole pan. P-e-r-f-e-c-t." She waved her fork. "This should put you in the finalist category."

Mary heaved a sigh. *"Danki."*

"Congratulations," Noah said as he walked past them and out the swinging door to the front of the store.

Amanda peered over her shoulder at the door. "What happened? Did you two get into a fight?"

"Nein. Yesterday, we dropped off some supplies at Lazy Susan's. We had a piece of

pie, and Bishop Yoder walked in and interrupted us. Noah left, and the bishop told me since I had been baptized and joined church, I shouldn't be dating an *Englischer*. Or what appeared that way."

"Mary, I'm sorry."

"*Nein*, it's for the best. We were getting too close, and it was going to lead to someone getting hurt. The bishop was right."

"What? I never thought I'd ever hear you say the bishop's advice was right. Did he say something to Noah, too? He's acting strange," Amanda whispered.

"Not that I know of. But I think by the look the bishop gave Noah, he got the idea I was in big trouble, and he should stay away. I'm moving the bakery out next week so it shouldn't be a problem."

"Okay, so we need to get busy. What time do you have to take the rolls over?"

"They have to be there by 2:00 p.m. So I need to get going." Mary carefully boxed up a dozen of her strawberry rolls. When she closed the kitchen door behind her, she paused.

Dear Heavenly Father, please bless my offering. I pray that it is a worthy entry and part of Your plan for me. Amen.

Noah rushed into the kitchen and looked around. Amanda stood at the sink, her back to him washing pans. "Where's Mary?" His words jumped out a bit too demanding.

Amanda jerked around. "She left to take her rolls over to be judged."

"When did she leave?"

"She just walked out the door. She had to hitch King, so she might still be at the corral. Why? Something wrong?"

"Jenny got a ride home from school to spend the weekend, but she borrowed the SUV to go visit friends. And I just noticed that I misread the judging time—it's not 3:00 p.m, it's 2:00 p.m. In fifteen minutes."

Amanda dried her hands and yelled. "Get your entry, and I'll run out and see if I can stop her."

He ran to the pantry, pulled a box off the shelf and set his banana cake inside. He darted out the door and headed across the street to the corral.

Mary was still waiting. "Hurry, Noah!" He climbed in, and before he could sit, she tapped the reins against King's back. The horse shot off down the street and threw Noah against the back of the seat. He righted himself and settled back, his hand still grasping the box. "Thanks for waiting."

Silence stretched across the buggy.

Finally, Mary glanced at him. "Yesterday, the bishop reminded me that I was a baptized member of the church. That means I have an obligation to my vow."

He nodded. "I understand."

Mary turned the buggy, set King at a fast trot down Ninth Street, pulled on the reins and stopped King by the contest booth. Noah jumped down, and Mary followed, grasping her entry.

When they reached the sidewalk next to the judging tent, Bishop Yoder was standing there watching them as they approached. Mary nodded to him and entered the tent behind Noah. They joined the registration line just as a contest worker closed the tent flap.

One glance at Mary's ashen face told Noah he'd gotten her into some serious trouble. "Thanks for the ride. I'll stay a while and find my own way home."

She nodded. *"Danki.* I'm sorry."

"No need to be. I understand." He regretted having to ask her for a ride.

On his way out of the tent, he spied Mary talking to the bishop.

The bishop glanced over Mary's shoulder at Noah with a stare that spoke volumes. Yes, he understood. He needed to stay away from her.

Early Friday morning, Mary unlocked the back door of the store and hung her bag. The kitchen had a strangeness hanging in the air. Noah stood at the counter stirring up something, and Amanda was at the sink washing dishes. Neither one greeted her. What was going on? As she headed to the pantry, Mary noticed the open newspaper on a chair. She glanced at it and stopped. The bold headline popped out.

Finalists Announced for the Kalona Fall Apple Festival Baking Contest

Her hand shook as she reached for the paper. The kitchen went silent. Mary drew in a deep breath as her eyes searched the column for the list of categories and winners.

1) Breads, rolls, scones:
Lilly Wiggs
Mary Brenneman
Timothy Jenkins

2) Pies, strudels, cakes:
Don Thompson
Noah Miller
Theresa Vogel

3) Cookies, cupcakes, bars:

Carlos Vegas
Clara Schnowsky
Cynthia Návar

Mary gasped. "Oh, no!"

"What's wrong, didn't you see your name?" Amanda hurried to her side.

"Yes, I see it, but one of the other finalists is Cynthia Návar. She's a pastry chef from Chicago, and she won the contest last year. Clara Schnowsky is a well-known chef from Des Moines."

Mary read the whole article then laid the paper back on the chair. "What are you making for the second round, Noah?"

"Apple strudel." He glanced up at her as he worked.

"*Gut*, I'm making apple bars."

"Don't worry." Amanda patted her shoulder. "You're a fabulous baker, and you can compete with the best of them."

"I hate dumping all the work on you."

"Nonsense. If you lose the bakery, I'm out of a job. I came in early because I knew you'd be a finalist in your category. So get baking, that cake will need to be perfect to take you to the final round."

"*Danki*, Amanda."

Noah opened the oven door, pulled out two dishes of apple strudel and set them in a corner to cool. "Amanda, I made two. When they cool, would you taste one and tell me what you think?"

"Of course, but aren't you afraid I might be biased?"

"That never occurred to me. Would you rather not do it since Mary is entering?"

"I'm only kidding. I'd love to taste yours. It smells *gut*, and I'll give you my honest opinion."

Heavy footfalls approached the kitchen from the grocery and Ethan poked his head around the doorway. "Here you are, Amanda. I thought you might be out front working." He sauntered up to her side, "Would you like to go to the festival with me tonight?"

Amanda smiled. "*Jah*, that would be nice."

"I'll stop back when you get off work."

"I'll be ready."

Ethan turned to leave but paused. "Noah, I thought you'd be out at your *grossdaddi*'s farm."

Noah lifted his head for a second but worked while he talked. "I've got a lot to do with all the festival baking, and I'm entered in the baking contest. What made you think I'd be at my grandpa's farm?"

Ethan's eyes widened. "I thought you knew. A cow was stuck in the mud. Your grandpa was out in the lot by himself and tried to help the old girl. The bossy lost her footing and fell on him. He lay there a long time. The bishop was called, and he told my *daed*."

Noah dropped the pan he was holding. "Is he dead?"

"*Nein*, but he's hurt bad. They think he broke his back. Your grandma went to look for him. When she found him, she called for help. He's in the hospital in Iowa City last I heard."

Noah tore off his apron and washed his hands. "Thanks for letting me know. When did it happen?"

"Yesterday, I think."

"Mary, I'm going to see my grandfather." His voice strained with concern.

"Okay, but what about your entry?"

He tossed her a glance. "When you go, would you mind entering it for me?" He grabbed his hat and keys off the hook that held them and headed for the back door.

"*Jah*, I can do that and pray." His sad eyes nearly squeezed the breath from her.

"*Danki* for stopping, Ethan. I'll see you later." Amanda patted his shoulder as he, too, headed for the back door.

"*Danki*, for bringing the news, Ethan. I know Noah really appreciated it." Mary recognized the look on Noah's face when he left. Sarah had a rough time having the twins and scared them all. Jah, she'd pray and keep her hands busy until he returned with the update on his *grossdaddi*.

She pulled the ingredients and stirred up

two pans of apple bars. While they baked, she cleaned up the kitchen and whipped cinnamon into the cream.

Amanda watched as the cream foamed nice and high. "Won't that melt before they get it judged?"

"I asked, and they said I can take the whipped cream in a small cooler, set it by the bars and add a note asking the judges to add the topping."

"You're taking a big chance with that idea." Amanda's voice held a skeptical warning.

"I know, but it's delicious. Have you tried Noah's strudel yet?"

"No. I'll try it right now." She sliced a piece and sat it on a plate. "It smells *gut.*" She took a bite, blinked then took another bite. Amanda looked at the strudel as if it had an odd taste.

"What's wrong? Isn't it fully baked?"

Amanda looked at Mary, her eyes as wide

as if she'd seen a bear. "It tastes as delicious as your apple strudel. In fact, it tastes like yours. Maybe better."

Chapter Nineteen

~⊂✦⊃~

Noah asked at the hospital's front desk for the room number of Thomas Miller. He found the room, knocked on the door and entered when his grandmother called, "Come in."

He slowly walked to his grandfather's bed. Cyrus and Judith were sitting in chairs off to the side by the window. Grandpa's eyes were open slightly, but his parted lips indicated he was ready for sleep.

Noah stood by the bed rail. "How do you feel? What happened? Ethan said a cow fell on you."

The old man looked frail. Days ago, when

Noah had visited, he'd looked healthy, strong, and even ten years younger. Now, just a few days later, age had caught up with him.

Grandpa's eyelids popped opened. "The cow's hooves had sunk in the mud, and she couldn't lift them out. When I tried to push her, she rocked back, slipped in the mud and pushed me down. She managed to get up off me, but I couldn't stand. My back hurt too badly. I managed to pull myself over to the gate and crawled through it, but I lay on the ground until Anna came." His eyes fluttered closed as if the talking had expended all his energy.

Noah sat in the chair beside his grandmother so he'd be close to the bed. He leaned toward her. "What's wrong with him? Did he break his back?"

"*Nein*, he was blessed. The Lord was with him and saw to it that he could maneuver out of the pen. He cracked three ribs. It hurts him to take deep breaths and move. They said six weeks to mend, but he will have restrictions on his activities. They're going to give him respiratory therapy to teach him breathing techniques to reduce the pain."

Noah leaned closer to the bed. "Grandpa, I'll come out and help you farm until you get healed."

Thomas tried to rise, then winced and fell back down. He gritted his teeth, gulped a breath and blew it out slowly. "Jeremiah never bothered to do his duty. You don't need to help me, either."

The words hit Noah like a wrecking ball, stunning him for a second. "I can't help what my dad did or how he treated you. That was between you and him."

Cyrus walked over to the bed. "Noah, I think it's time you left. He doesn't need all this stress and strain. You're not wanted here."

Noah scanned his grandfather's face. "I love you and want to help no matter what you think. I don't know why Dad left you to do the work by yourself, but it doesn't sound like him. Dad worked day and night in the store. He was a dedicated, hardworking man." Noah swallowed hard. "The man you talk about wasn't the man I knew. Maybe he matured over the years. But I loved him, and I'm willing to forgive as God says I must do. Everyone says you Amish are gentle and forgiving, but I don't see it. You're vindictive, spiteful and unforgiving."

Cyrus moved a step closer to Noah. "I think it's time you left." He pointed to the door.

"I want to talk to Noah. Sit down, Cyrus, and don't interfere." Grandpa glanced up and put one hand on the bed railing. "The family jumped to conclusions the day your father left. Except, he didn't just leave. I threw him off the property and told him never to come back. Jeremiah had been working with my father at his bakery. The bakery that Joshua Lapp, Sarah Brenneman's *daed*, and my father owned for a short time together. Jeremiah told me that morning on the barn roof that he didn't want to farm with me. He wanted to own a store and bakery. He said

Cyrus and I could farm together. Cyrus and I have never seen eye to eye on anything."

Cyrus let out a loud huff but never said a word.

Grandpa gripped the railing and took another breath. "I told Jeremiah to get off the farm and never come back. He did just that. I never saw him again. I'm ashamed of myself." His voice trailed off, and tears streamed down the old man's cheek. He finally brushed them away with a trembling hand.

Noah stood and strolled closer to the old man's bed. His grandpa's eyelids fluttered shut then opened and shut again. "Grandpa," he said quietly, "I'm going to go so you can sleep, but I'll be back tomorrow."

The old man's head nodded slightly.

Closing the door, Noah rested his back against it for a few seconds, trying to absorb a new truth. He pushed himself away, his knees trembling, but he managed the distance to his vehicle.

Noah rested his hands on the steering

wheel, letting the amazement of his grand-father's confession wash over him. He slid the gearshift to Drive, hit the gas and eased out into traffic. He thanked God all the way back to Kalona for finally lifting the veil and revealing the truth.

He squeezed the steering wheel as another truth swirled around in his heart. He should have been Amish instead of *Englisch*. Everything that he was familiar and comfortable with his whole life was a lie.

Mary rushed to drop off her bars and Noah's strudel at the judging tent and raced back to get started practicing for the last round, in case she won this round. Her hands shook as she pulled her pie out of the oven. Amanda said Noah's strudel was better than hers and that made her nervous.

Amanda stepped back. "Be careful you don't drop that. Is something wrong?"

"I'm afraid my pie won't have an exceptional enough taste to win the contest."

"*Nein.* Stop doubting yourself. You are

every bit as *gut* as Noah. You can do this." Amanda cheered as she dried a plate.

Ethan burst through the kitchen door. "Sorry, I'm late, Amanda, I got held up doing chores. The buggy is waiting out back."

"I'll be there in a minute."

Mary's gaze shifted from the door to Amanda. "Ethan really is taking you to the festival then?"

"*Nein*, he's not taking me, we're just going together."

"I heard him ask you. It sounded like a date to me."

Amanda finished drying dishes and putting them away. "He's never really called me a *freundin*, but I'll soon be twenty-one, an old maid. He might just be hanging around waiting for Jenny to show up so he can talk to her." Her voice quaked.

Mary cocked her head at her friend. "How do you feel about that?"

"It hurts if I let myself think about it. It

hurts a lot. But the only reason it hurts is because I like him."

"Maybe you should ask him about your relationship and where it's going."

Amanda headed for the door and stopped. "Because I'm scared of the answer."

"So you're hoping that if you go out enough, you'll grow on him?"

"*Jah*, but it sounded better when I first thought of it."

Mary rushed across the kitchen and gave Amanda a hug. "Don't get hurt."

"*Nein*, I'm tough, and in spite of the situation, we have a *gut* time together. Do you want to go with us?"

"*Danki*, but I'll catch up with you and Ethan in a little while."

Mary finished cleaning the kitchen then glanced at the clock. 5:45 p.m. It was almost time for them to read the names of the winners of the second round. The winners of each category would compete tomorrow for the grand prize.

She gathered her bag, locked the front

door of the store and stepped to the side-walk just as Noah pulled his SUV up to the curb and rolled down the window. "Need a lift to the festival?"

"Danki." She opened the door and slid onto the seat. "How's your *grossdaddi*?"

"He's got three cracked ribs. He can't do much for the next six weeks, but he'll heal. Are you excited about hearing who won?"

"I'm nervous. Cynthia Návar, the chef from Chicago, won last year, and she's here again this year."

"You're a wonderful baker, Mary. Don't let Cynthia intimidate you. Keep your eye on your goal. Don't let anyone steal your vision."

"You're right. Let's change the subject. Who is going to do Thomas's farming?"

"Since you, Amanda and Jean do such a good job watching the store, I thought I could go out to the farm for a while each day and help. It's the end of September, tourism will start to slow down, and that will give me time to help my grandpa. I thought sometimes Emily could come along and help grandma."

"Of course we can do that for you and Thomas."

Noah pulled up by the curb and stopped. "I'll let you off here and go park."

Mary slid out of the vehicle and gazed at all the festivalgoers, tents, game booths, activities, and food wagons. There were more in attendance this year than ever before. Maybe the feuding and the increased prize for the baking contest had drawn more people. She pushed her way through the crowd and walked straight into Bishop Yoder.

"*Gut* day, Mary."

A swarm of butterflies rampaged her stomach. "*Hallo*, Bishop. A *wunderbaar* festival, *jah*?"

He nodded. "Mary, can I have a word with you?"

"Of course. Is something wrong?"

He walked her to the edge of the sidewalk. "Some members of the *Gmay* have contacted me regarding all this commotion about the feud between you and Noah Miller. It's causing attention and drawing this huge crowd here to see who will win the prize of $20,000, a trophy and a trip to New York. You have made a spectacle of the Amish people. Your name appeared in the newspaper along with the mention of our Plain community. Only we don't seem so Plain when you have all those fancy pastries in your bakery and on display in a contest. The *Gmay* has decided to forbid you to participate any further in this contest."

Mary gasped. "Bishop, they can't do that."

Daed and *Mamm*, holding the twins, walked up behind the bishop and stood off to the side. "What's going on here?" *Daed* asked, his gaze flinging from Mary to the bishop.

"Your *tochter* will tell you, Caleb. It's time she acted like she is Plain." Bishop Yoder turned and stomped off down the sidewalk.

Mary clutched her quilted bag and twisted the straps around her hand. *Jah*, she knew what the bishop meant. Not only did she have to give up the contest and maybe the chance to save the bakery, but he was expecting her to give up her relationship with Noah. She hadn't wanted to admit it before, but she loved Noah.

Chapter Twenty

Mary walked beside her *stiefmutter*, delaying any lecture from *Daed*, as her gaze scanned the area for Noah.

"What's going on, Mary, why was the bishop so upset?" Sarah waved her hand in the direction of the bishop storming off then wrapped her arm back around Liza.

Daed walked up on Mary's other side. "What did you do? No doubt it has something to do with Noah. As soon as the festival is over, it's time for you to move back to Sweet Delights. It should be ready to open in a couple of weeks."

Sarah nodded in agreement. "Mayor Conrad told us that this year the festival has broken an all-time attendance record. He said it's because of the publicized feud between you and Noah, which was also the reason why they raised the prize money to $20,000. Is that what's bothering the bishop?"

Mary lowered her head as Sarah's words galloped over her like a runaway horse. She gulped a breath. "*Jah*, but it sounds like the town should be thanking us."

"The town is praising you and Noah, but the bishop is upset with all the notoriety and attention a member is bringing to his Community. We are a Plain, quiet people. Having the news media say an Amish woman has an opportunity to win money, a trophy and a trip to New York City doesn't sound Plain or quiet," her vater chided.

"You can't accept a *trophy*. The bishop is looking out for our church," *Mamm* softly chastised.

"I know, it was never supposed to blow up into this big of a deal." Mary threw her arms open and gestured to the park bursting with tents and festivalgoers.

"What's going on between you and the store owner?" *Daed* tilted his head toward Noah standing at the contest tent motioning for her to come over there.

"Nothing. I work at his store. That's all. You two are imagining things." Mary slipped her arm around her *mamm* and pulled her over to the quilt tent.

She walked beside *mamm* up and down aisles while *Daed* followed behind with Lena squirming in his arms wanting to get down.

Mary turned to look at a quilt behind her and noticed Amanda and Ethan hurrying toward her.

Amanda caught Mary's arm. "Come, they are getting ready to read the names of the finalists."

"*Ach*, I didn't realize the time." She turned to Sarah. "They are going to read the names of the finalists. I'm going with Amanda to the contest tent."

Mamm nodded. "Go, we'll see you there."

Mary followed Amanda and Ethan and as she approached the contest tent, she watched for a glimpse of Noah but couldn't find him.

Inside the contest tent, Amanda weaved her way through the throng of people to the front by the podium. Mary searched the faces of the crowd. Off in the corner, Noah stood talking to Cynthia Návar, the chef from Chicago.

The loud speaker squawked. "Good afternoon, everyone, I'm Connie Goodnight. We are so pleased to see such a great turnout for our festival and participation in the baking contest. Just a refresher of the rules before I announce the names. It is mandatory that all three, category winners bake their final entry in front of the judges. They will evaluate and assign points on degree of difficulty, originality, presentation and taste."

Whispers and shuffling of feet sounded throughout the tent. Connie tapped on the microphone for quiet. "The names I read will be the finalists, who will meet tomorrow at 10:00 a.m. at Lazy Susan's. The contestants must bring everything they need to make their dessert. They will receive the use of the restaurant's stoves, ovens and refrigerators. Good baking to you all and please hold your applause until all three names are announced. Category one, Mary Brenneman. Category two, Noah Miller. Category three, Cynthia Návar."

The tent erupted into applause.

Amanda grabbed Mary and squeezed her in a hug. "You did it, but I knew you would."

Ethan patted her shoulder. "Congrats, Mary. You deserve it. I'll be rooting for you."

"*Danki*, Ethan." A rush of excitement soared through her, and tears clouded her vision as she blinked them away. She drew a choked breath. "I'm so excited I'm going back to the store right now to get my supplies ready to take to Lazy Susan's. I don't want to forget a thing." I'll deal with the bishop later.

"Amanda and I'll give you a ride back," Ethan offered.

"*Danki* but you two stay. It's only a few blocks, and I want to walk off this energy and clear my head."

Mamm and *Daed* had waited for her by the tent opening. "Congratulations, *honig*. We are so happy for you." *Mamm* patted her cheek.

"*Danki* but the bishop isn't. He said the *Gmay* has forbidden me from competing any further in the contest. What will they do if I continue?"

Mamm looked at *Daed*, then leveled her gaze back on Mary. "He will probably discipline you. You may have to apologize in front of the congregation."

"Is that all?"

Daed placed a hand on Sarah's shoulder. "Mary, if the bishop has warned you, he will take action. If they find you in violation of a biblical teaching, you may have to go before the *Gmay* to confess or explain your behavior. Be careful, *tochter*, it's a serious matter."

"I asked permission to enter, and the bishop said I could. Now that the news media has made a story out of Noah and me, and they printed my name in the paper, our community is upset. I can't control that."

Sarah's voice turned dire. "Mary, you need to talk to the bishop and the *Gmay*. They don't like the attention that's being given to the Plain community."

"*Mamm*, the final contest is tomorrow. There isn't time to ask permission. Just because my name was mentioned in the newspaper, it doesn't go against biblical teaching or the *Ordnung*. Gossiping and bringing false accusation against another member is also a biblical teaching."

"Be careful, Mary. You need to think about your actions." *Daed* pressed his hand on Sarah's back and guided her down the sidewalk. "We'll see you at home."

"Congratulations, Mary." Noah tapped her shoulder.

She jerked and whirled around. "*Jah*, to you, too. We did it. I can hardly believe we made it into the final contest." She caught control of her wavering voice.

"Is everything all right?"

"I—I'm not sure. The bishop told me our *Gmay* is concerned about all the publicity I've been receiving. They said it looks bad for the Plain community and have forbidden me to bake tomorrow."

Noah laughed. "Really, who is saying that? I was over at the Amish wood-crafting shop, and they told me business is booming with all the tourist and festivalgoers in town this week. They also said the Plain community bakery in the country is doing very well."

"Are you teasing me, Noah?"

"No, that's what they said. Did he say the names of those complaining?"

"*Nein*, but I'll ask next time and repeat what you told me."

"Are you going back to the bakery? I can

give you a ride." He motioned to his vehicle parked a few hundred feet away.

"*Danki*, but I'm in enough trouble. Besides, I want to walk and think though this mess before I make a decision." She crossed the street and headed down the sidewalk.

Maybe someone was jealous of her chance to win $20,000. Jealousy and envy were also against biblical teachings.

Mary unlocked the back door of the store and was surprised not to see Noah. She hung her bag and found his note. "I'll let you work alone, and I'll pack later. N."

She pulled a box out of the pantry for her supplies to take to Lazy Susan's. As she practiced making a pie, she washed and placed each bowl, measuring spoon, whisk and ingredients in the box. She made a copy of her recipe and placed that in. When the pie cooled, she sat down, drew a deep breath and took a big bite… Perfect.

Mary grabbed her box out of Noah's store on Saturday morning and hurried to Lazy

Susan's. After a sleepless night, she was running late and Amanda said Noah had already left for the restaurant.

When she knocked, Simone opened the door and led her to the kitchen. Noah and Cynthia had already arrived and set up their workstations.

Mary nodded as she passed them, following Simone to her area. She set her box down, and laid out all her utensils and ingredients on her station as Chef Simone André instructed.

Simone watched the clock. "Five minutes, chefs."

Mary blotted her hands on her apron, drew a deep breath and prayed.

"It's ten o'clock. You have four hours. Go!" Simone yelled.

Mary simmered fresh spices in apple juice, added the sugar, and thickened it. She made the crust, peeled and sliced the apples. She arranged them piled high in the shell then poured the spice mixture over top. She set the pie in the warmed oven and set the timer. While that baked, she made the caramel sauce. When the pie came out of the oven, she set it to cool then added the warm caramel sauce.

Simone called a thirty-minute warning, then ten. "Stop. Please bring your desserts to the judges' table in the restaurant area."

Mary led the way into the restaurant, set her dish down in front of the judges, took a step back and waited for Noah and Cynthia to follow suite.

"Thank you, contestants, your jobs are done. You may go and enjoy the festival. The winner to the baking contest winner will be announced at four o'clock." Simone smiled and waved her hand toward the door.

Mary stepped out the door, her heart pounding like a sledgehammer, and drew a deep breath. "I'm glad that's over."

Noah and Cynthia followed her out, stopped and heaved big sighs.

"Would you two ladies like me to give you a ride back to the festival?" Noah's gaze bounced from Mary to Cynthia.

"Thank you, but my husband, Brian, is waiting for me." Cynthia slipped her cell phone back in her pocket as she approached the car at the curb. She turned back to Mary and Noah. "See you at the announcement."

Noah fell into step beside Mary. "It seems we're always together, and I get the impression your family doesn't like it."

"I'm going to meet Amanda and Ethan at the festival, but I'll walk. My family is protective of me. They don't want to see me get hurt again by someone who doesn't have my best interests at heart."

Her words walloped Noah's chest. He fought to take a deep breath. Seth had hurt Mary deeply, that was obvious. While she walked back to the festival, he hurried to the store and entered the backdoor to the kitchen. The steamy heat of fresh-baked peanut butter bars wafted through the air. "Mmm, the bars smell good."

Emily held up a plate. "They're all ready for the contest. Jenny helped me."

"Well, sort of." Jenny hugged her little sister. "Emily really knew what she was doing. I was impressed. Amanda and Mary did a great job of teaching our little girl how to bake." Jenny beamed with pride.

Emily set her plate down and covered it with plastic wrap. "Thanks for coming home, Jenny, to watch me compete in the contest, Noah, are you going over to the festival with Jenny and me?"

"I wouldn't miss it, little sister, but we need to get going." Noah stopped at the checkout counter in the front of the store. "Jean, if I'm not back by six o'clock, go ahead and lock up."

She nodded. "Have fun."

At the park, Jenny excused herself to find friends, and Noah guided Emily to the judging tent and helped her register her entry. "Shall we walk around and come back later for the contest results?"

"Yes, but I'm really nervous, Noah. All the other entries looked yummy."

But Emily forgot about her entry by the

time they reached the first game booth. She tried to knock over bottles with a tennis ball to win a prize. "I'm not a good ball thrower."

"I'm not either, Emily. I spend my time baking, not throwing a ball."

Noah followed his sister around the festival from booth to booth. At the next booth, she caught a plastic, floating duck and won a hair barrette. While she picked out her prize, Noah glanced at his watch. "Let's hurry back to the judging tent and find chairs before they're all gone."

They found their seats. Five minutes later, Noah watched Emily squirm around on her chair. She jumped up and stood then flopped back down. When Goodnight walked to the podium and tapped on the microphone, Noah grabbed Emily's hand and squeezed. She glanced up at him and smiled. Their mom would have been so proud of her little girl so grown up and baking.

"We will announce the three finalists' names to the children's bakeoff in no particular order. You can all come forward, but audience, please hold your applause until all the names are read." Connie glanced at her paper. "Roger Ferguson, Summer Conway, Emily Miller."

Emily flew off the chair and ran to the front. Noah smiled and blotted a tear at the corner of his eye as the tent erupted into applause.

Finally, Connie raised her hand for quiet. "Again, please hold your applause until all names and places have been read, they receive their certificates and first place gets their pink backpack. In third place, Summer Conway. Second place winner, Roger Ferguson. And first place winner, Emily Miller."

The tent roared with clapping and cheers. Noah jumped from his seat, pushed his way to the front, grabbed Emily and hugged her. "I'm so proud of you."

"Noah, I didn't think I could do it! I would have been happy winning third place. I can't believe I actually got first place. Now I want to start working for you in the bakery. I could make my peanut butter bars and cookies and—"

"Slow down." Noah laughed. "You can make a few things, but don't forget you're still in school."

"I know, I'm just so excited!"

"Emily!" Kate, Emily's friend, squealed as she ran up and hugged her. "You won. I'm so proud of you. Now you can teach me to bake better. My folks are waiting for me, do you want to come and walk around the festival with us?"

Noah nodded his approval. "If you can't find me when you're done, go back to the store, and I'll be there at six when Jean leaves."

"Okay, Noah." Emily grabbed Kate's hand, and they ran off through the crowd.

The microphone squawked, and Connie held her hand up. "Please take your seats. We need to make the presentation for the main baking contest." She waited for the tent to quiet down.

Noah found his seat and looked around for Mary. He saw Cynthia sitting next to the tent wall on the opposite side with her husband. She waved and gave Noah a thumbs-up.

Mary pushed her way past a couple of people waiting for chairs. "Is this seat taken?" she asked him.

Noah moved his arm from the back of the chair. "I was saving it for you. Did you see Emily win?"

She slid around Noah and sat down. "Yes, Amanda, Ethan and I were in the back with Jenny. I caught Emily on her way out. She's ecstatic over her win. I'm so happy for her. It gave her a boost of confidence."

"I'll say. Now she wants to bake for me."

"She's old enough to help. I baked at her age."

Connie put her hand in the air, motioning for quiet. When the crowd finally simmered down, she glanced down at the paper in her hand. After a few seconds, she leveled her gaze at the audience. "This year's contest has turned out to have a very unusual result." She waved her hand toward the table with the desserts from the three finalists.

"But first, let me introduce our panel of judges. Magdalena Morgan from Magdalena's Pastry Shop, Chicago, Illinois. Joel Bélanger from Bélanger French Cuisine, Des Moines, Iowa. And Simone André from MyBaking Channel.

A round of applause acknowledged the judges.

A voice directly behind Mary broke through the noise. "Hope one of you two show them how it's done in Iowa."

Mary smiled. *"Danki,* Frank."

Connie motioned for the crowd to simmer down. "Next, let's have our three finalists come up front. I will call names in no particular order. Cynthia Návar, Mary Brenneman and Noah Miller."

She held up a hand for the clapping to stop. "According to the rules, the judges were to select a finalist based on degree of difficulty, originality, presentation and taste.

However, the judges have told me there is a clear third place, but two of the dishes met all the criteria and their numbers added up to the same score."

Murmurs from the crowd grew louder as she tried to talk. Connie raised her voice. "Please, just give me a few more minutes to explain. Two desserts were so close in taste that it was impossible to tell which was best. In fact, the tastes seem identical. It was brought to our attention that these two dishes are from contestants who are friends and who work together."

Mary gasped and turned toward Noah. "You stole my recipe?"

Her words flamed across the space between them and seared into Noah's gut.

Chapter Twenty-One

Mary whirled to her side and faced Noah. "Did you use my recipe without asking? I trusted you." Her heart nearly fell to the floor.

Noah gasped. "I didn't take your recipe. I used mine."

"Please," Connie interrupted, "can either of you explain how this happened?"

Whispers and voices hummed throughout the tent.

Connie tapped the mic. "We need quiet."

Mary's legs froze to the spot as humiliation raised bile to her throat. She spotted her *stiefmutter* and *daed* with red tinging their faces.

"I didn't steal your recipe," Noah went on. "It's in my family recipe book. I don't make it often because it's time-consuming, although delicious. It's been in my family for at least four generations, maybe longer."

Old Bishop Ropp pushed his way to the front. He stomped up to the dessert table, picked up a spoon and tasted both of the dishes. "Mary, this is the pie I was telling you about that Sarah's vater used to make when he was in partnership with Miller."

Sarah Brenneman rushed up to the front. "What are you talking about, Bishop? My father never had a partner."

"Yes, he did when he first opened before you were born. The partnership didn't last very long, and the two men weren't friends after that."

Sarah gasped. "My *daed* never told me any story like that."

Anna Miller stepped forward. "Yes, I remember hearing my father-in-law talking about those days. Remember, Noah, Thomas told you yesterday that his *daed* had a partnership with Joshua Lapp, and that Sweet Delights was the bakery they owned together?"

Sarah shook her head. "That's funny because *daed* never mentioned it. How long were they in business, and why did they split up?

Anna placed a finger to her temple. "They had some sort of a disagreement. They couldn't work it out so they split up. Sweet Delights is the bakery they started together. Thomas might know more of the details."

"So," Connie broke in, "am I to understand that these two desserts are from the same recipe?"

"It appears they are." Mary glanced at Noah.

Noah nodded. "It seems the recipes are the same."

Connie grabbed the microphone. "To state it for the audience and the news media, there is no stipulation against two people entering the same baked good, although it is usually done as one entry. Do you two want to count your entries as one so we can declare a winner? Otherwise, I'm not sure how we would declare a winner."

Noah whispered to Mary, and she nodded.

Mary stammered and cleared her throat. "Under these unusual circumstances, Noah and I agree to combine are entries as one and accept the check together, but we would like to give Cynthia the trophy and the spot on the cable channel."

Connie looked at Simone, who nodded. "Simone agrees to that. Cynthia, if you'll come forward."

Cynthia thanked Mary and Noah as she strolled over and stood by Connie.

Connie lifted the trophy from the stand and handed it to Cynthia. "The Kalona Fall Apple Festival baking contest presents you with this trophy," and the invitation to appear on the Simone André Show on My-Baking Channel."

After the applauding quieted, Connie motioned to Mary and Noah. "Please come forward."

Mary glanced at Noah as they took a step forward.

"As the winner of the first place entry, I want to award you this check for $20,000." The tent erupted into a commotion. Connie let it continue for a while then tapped the mic. "I want to thank all who participated in the baking contest and hope to see you next year."

Mary grabbed Noah's arm. "Let's get Sarah and Anna and go outside and talk."

He nodded. "I'll get Anna and meet you on the sidewalk."

When he approached with his grandmother outside, Mary faced him. "So you knew about the joint business all along?"

He stopped so fast he stubbed his toe on the sidewalk. "I knew that my great-grandfather co-owned a bakery in the beginning. I didn't find out it was Sarah's dad until yesterday at the hospital when my grandpa told me. I didn't have a chance to tell you."

He looked at Anna. "Can you explain more about the bakeries?"

"*Jah,* after they had their disagreement, Sarah's *daed* bought out Thomas's father. He didn't feel there was enough business in Kalona for two bakeries and moved to Iowa City and established his bakery there." Anna shrugged. "That's all I know. You could ask Thomas. He might remember."

"Why is it that I never knew all this, Anna? No one ever talked about it," Sarah pressed.

"It was before you were born and most have probably forgotten about it. Aaron Miller moved his bakery to Iowa City and was in a different district than us, so you probably never saw him, Sarah. It's funny your *daed* never had an occasion to bring it up." Anna raised a brow.

Sarah shook her head. "I can't believe Daed never told me."

Noah interrupted. "But, Grandma, if my dad learned baking from Aaron, how did he travel that distance to work in his bakery?"

"After your great-grandfather's wife died, he fell and broke his leg, and Jeremiah moved in with him in Iowa City for about a year. He actually didn't want to go home, but Thomas made him because he wanted Jeremiah to take over the farm. Then Aaron died. After your daed left home, he started his own bakery."

Sarah put her arm around Mary. "Congratulations, *honig*. I'm going to go find your *vater* and *bruder* and walk around the festival with them for a while. We'll see you at home."

"I'm going back to the festival, too, Noah, unless you have more questions." Anna turned toward the park.

"Thanks, Grandma. You were very helpful. Do you need a ride home?"

"*Nein*, Cyrus and Lois are here, they'll take me home. And I have just enough time to visit the quilt tent." Anna smiled as she headed that way.

"Noah, I want to apologize for not trusting you." Mary's heart ached with regret.

"No, Mary, it's I who should be apologizing to you. Trust is a two-way street. It was an important piece of information that you didn't know, and I didn't take the time to tell you. I'm sorry. I was busy and going to tell you later. To be honest, I never thought anything like this could happen." His amber eyes sparkled at her.

"Yes, it was a total surprise for me, too."

He motioned to his SUV parked nearby. "Do you want a ride back to the store to get your buggy?"

"That would be nice. I'm still shaking from all the excitement."

As Mary turned toward Noah's SUV, Bishop Yoder and Rebecca strolled by on the sidewalk toward their buggy. *Jah*, he'd be paying her a visit tomorrow and would probably want her confession. But she had his approval to enter for the chance of winning $10,000 and that's all she won.

But what would she say about Noah? She'd told the bishop that she knew what her baptism meant. Yet how could she confess from her heart when that meant staying away from Noah? Could she keep that promise?

She had to, and that meant choosing a man from her faith. No doubt, the bishop would mention Seth again.

Tears filled her eyes as fast as she could blink them away.

Gott, You said You would bless me with joy and You would lead my feet on the right path, but where are You? My heart is breaking, and my joy is spilling out. Noah is my joy. I can't be Englisch, *and he's not willing to become Amish. Where is Your healing balm for my breaking heart?*

Noah walked Mary to his vehicle, opened the door and helped her in. As she passed by, he drew a deep breath of her honeysuckle hair. Her fragrance nearly melted his heart.

He drove to the corral and parked. "I'll help you hitch King. Then I'm going to Iowa

City to pick up my grandpa and take him home."

"Are they releasing him?"

"Yes, but he has to be careful. I told him I'd be out to help him so he didn't have to worry about the farm."

"That's nice of you. I can hitch King. You can get going."

"Nonsense, it'll only take a few minutes."

Noah tightened the girth and finished hitching King feeling Mary's eyes on his back as he worked.

"Noah, I can tell you've been working at your grandpa's farm. You hitched King a lot faster than I thought you would." She stepped into the buggy. "*Danki.* Just so you know… I'm going to terminate my temporary shop at your store so you can get the space back to normal. Sweet Delights is ready for interior work, and I want to be there and help. Also, the bishop seeing us at lunch and together in your store gives the impression that we have some kind of relationship. I'm a baptized member of our church." Her voice wobbled before she gained control. "I have pledged my devotion to Jesus and to my community, and it doesn't look right for me to spend so much time with an *Englischer*." She shook the reins. "Giddyap, King."

Noah stepped away from the buggy and watched as the only woman he'd ever loved drove out of sight and out of his heart. His stomach did flips when she was near and felt as empty as a rain gauge in the middle of July when she left.

He swiped his hand down the side of his vehicle. What would make a man give up this type of automation and turn to driving a horse and buggy?

Staring down the road after Mary, he let a smile stretch across his face. One fine woman that he knew his life would never be the same without. But she wasn't the only reason.

Noah started his SUV and headed in the direction of Bishop Yoder's house. He turned in the driveway, parked and gripped the steering wheel while he said a prayer. Since he had met Mary, he'd relied on prayer and trusted God a lot more.

Enough stalling. He pushed himself out, marched to the bishop's front door and knocked. No answer. He knocked again. Were they still at the fall festival? He turned to leave just as the door opened.

The bishop glared at Noah with a puzzled look on his face.

"Bishop Yoder, may I speak to you?"

"What is this regarding?" His words had a tart sound.

"I understand it is up to you to decide if I'm sincere in my request to become Amish, and I ask for your permission."

The bishop's eyes widened. His back straightened with a startled jerk. "Come in." He stepped back. "We just returned from the festival and my feet are tired, so I hope this won't take long." He led the way to his office, closed the door and motioned to a chair. "So what is this all about?"

"I want to join the Amish church." Noah firmed his shoulders and spoke decisively.

Bishop Yoder fell back into his chair and stared at Noah. "Why do you want to join our community? Is it because you want to wed Mary?

"We aren't seeing each other, no matter what you think. I do love her and would like to court her. Whether she says yes or no, I still want to join and be part of my family's community."

The bishop leaned back in his chair. "You would need to study the church rules, learn Pennsylvania Dutch and dress like the members of our community." He nodded. "I have some clothes here that might fit you. Tomorrow is Church Sunday, your *grossdaddi* and his family are hosting."

The bishop stood and walked briskly to the door. He opened it and stepped into the hall. "Rebecca, would you bring that extra suit from the closet?" His voice lowered. "The one that fits me a little snug. There is someone here who needs to borrow it."

With suit in hand, Noah followed the bishop down the hall to the front door.

"We'll talk later, after you've had time to see if this is what you really want. There will also be classes. And don't forget, you'll need a horse and buggy." His tone at the end told Noah he enjoyed saying that immensely.

Noah turned, smiled at the bishop and nodded. Yes, it would be worth it to be part of his Amish family and try for the chance to win Mary's heart.

He certainly hadn't expected this turn of events. But weren't God's surprises the best kind? Had God told him His plan earlier, Noah might never have come to Kalona. But he was sure glad God had set his feet on Route 218.

Mary followed her *stiefmutter* into Thomas Miller's new barn on Church Sunday, and slid onto the bench next to Sarah. She caught sight of a man entering the building. He walked to the men's side and found a spot on the bench. He looked familiar, but his hat shaded his face.

When the singing started, the man took off his hat, leaned over, placed it under the bench and straightened back up. Mary gasped and threw her hand over her mouth.

"What's wrong, Mary?" Sarah whispered.

"Look straight across, last row. It's Noah Miller."

Sarah glanced over and smiled. "He's been seeing quite a lot of his grandparents and helping Thomas on the farm, *jah*?"

"Did you know about this, *Mamm*?"

"*Nein*, but Anna did say how helpful and *wunderbaar* the *bu* was and said they were becoming fond of him."

Mary's mind wandered to Noah during the introductory message, but when the preacher started the main sermon, he dwelled on two points, the ones they often emphasized for a new member.

The first, "be not conformed to this world," Romans 12:2; and the second, "be ye not unequally yoked together with unbelievers,"

2 Corinthians 6:14. This one, the preacher explained, forbade an Amish person from marrying or entering a business partnership with a non-Amish person.

Mary's throat welled with a lump. She'd hadn't expected to see Noah in Amish clothing. What had made him decide to take such a big step?

She looked for Noah after service but couldn't find him. She'd caught sight of him at the table but there wasn't time to talk. After the common-meal cleanup, Mary started across the lawn to meet her parents at their buggy. When she crossed the driveway, there sat Noah under the tree sitting on a swing. He stood and met her halfway.

"Hello, Mary."

"Noah, what a surprise. What changed your mind?"

"Emily has been going out to our grandparents' farm with me. She has met several Amish girl cousins, and they have become friends. Together, we made the decision."

Mary glanced at her *daed* waiting in the buggy. "I need to go."

"Mary, I have one thing to ask." He paused. "I would like to court you. You'll probably want to think about it."

Tears blurred her eyes. She pressed a fingertip against each one. "*Nein*, I don't need to think about it." A smile brewed deep in her stomach and burst across her face. "*Jah*, I would like that very much."

"I borrowed Ethan's buggy. Can I give you a ride home?"

"I'll run and tell *Daed*."

When she returned, Noah walked her to his buggy. She settled on the seat a foot from the man she wanted to marry. She could feel his warmth just inches from her. Noah reached across the expanse and took her hand in his, her heart beating faster by the moment.

She turned toward Noah as he shook the reins and turned the buggy down the drive and out onto the road.

Noah winked. "I was worried you

wouldn't say yes." He guided the buggy to the side of the road and stopped. He pulled her into his arms, his face bathed in a smile so *wunderbaar* it stole her heart.

He lowered his lips to hers for a tender kiss. "I love you, Mary, with all my heart. I never want to let you out of my arms."

"*Ich liebe dich*, I love you, Noah Miller." She drew in a deep, shuddering breath as his lips touched hers once again. *Jah*, he was the man she wanted to marry, and she'd spend the rest of her life making him forget the *Englisch* ways.

Epilogue

One year later

After returning with Noah from their twenty-minute premarital talk with the ministers, Mary sat next to her attendants, side-sitters Amanda and Nettie. Heat burning her cheeks remembering the ministers' words as they explained what it meant to be a *frau* and *ehemann*.

Her heart pulsed with an overwhelming love for Noah, sitting on the bench parallel to hers. His attendants Ethan and Jacob, sitting next to him. She'd always remember this moment, and how her love bubbled over for this man.

The three-hour service focused on marital relationship, the obstacles, the joys, and working together to raise a family. The bishop gave examples of biblical marriages and walking the road of a *frau that* were inspirational.

Her heart raced and her throat tightened as the time to take her vow drew near. She blotted her hands together.

"Mary, calm down. You look like you're ready to faint," Amanda whispered.

She winked at Amanda and her cousin Nettie. "I'm fine, just nervous."

Bishop Yoder rose and walked to the front of her daed's barn. "Noah and Mary, will you please join me?"

Mary rose and walked beside Noah to stand before the bishop.

"Will you join hands?" the bishop said with a soft voice.

"Are you willing to enter into wedlock as God ordained?" the bishop asked.

"Yes," they replied in unison.

"Noah, do you believe *Gott* has ordained Mary to be your wedded *frau*?"

"Yes."

"Mary, do you believe *Gott* has ordained Noah to be your wedded *ehemann*?"

Her throat grew dry and tight as tears teetered at the edges of her eyelids. "Yes."

The bishop placed a warm palm over her and Noah's clasped hands. The bishop's voice was rich and reverent. "May the *Gott* of Abraham, the *Gott* of Isaac and the *Gott* of Jacob be with you and bless you abundantly through Jesus Christ. I now pronounce you *ehemann* and *frau*."

After the service, Noah grabbed her hands and pulled her close. "Now you are all mine for the rest of our lives," then he smiled. "But right now, my lovely frau, we must greet our guests."

Jenny and Emily threw their arms around

Mary. "Welcome to the family, Mary. You look lovely." Jenny crushed her new sister-in-law to her then stepped back and let Emily hug Mary.

"We're sisters now, Mary." Emily beamed. "Jenny helped me make a cake for the *Eck,* the bridal table. It's the tall vanilla one with lots of frosting."

"*Danki,* I'm so proud of you. I will make sure I have a piece of it. I'm going to enjoy having sisters to talk to and share my secrets with." Mary squeezed Emily again.

Jenny grabbed Emily's hand and tugged her away. "We'll go get our places and see you at dinner."

As wedding guests started to drift toward the dinner tables, Noah leaned close to her ear and whispered, "Come, Mary. I have something to show you." He tightened his grip on her hand, pulling her across the lawn over the driveway and toward his buggy.

"Stop, Noah! We can't leave our own wedding."

He laughed. "Mrs. Miller, I would sure like to, but instead, I have a wedding gift for you. Stand right here, close your eyes and hold your hands out. Wait just a minute." There was a rustling sound from his buggy, and then something soft and heavy was laid in her arms. "Okay, open your eyes."

Mary blinked and dropped her jaw. Tears filled her eyes. It was the quilt her real *mamm* had made her. "Where did you get it?"

"Sarah saw it sticking out of your bag after she told you they couldn't afford to give you the thousand dollars for an espresso machine. She figured you took it to the consignment shop. It upset her. And when she stopped into my store to see what you were competing against, she told me."

Mary wrapped her arms around him, squeezing the quilt between them. "*Danki*, Noah. You'll never know how much my heart hurt that day or how much it is filled today knowing you are my *ehemann*."

A man huffed and puffed as he ran toward

them, his feet scuffing the stones on the driveway. Noah released his hold on Mary and turned.

"Oh, no you don't. You're not leaving your own wedding just yet." Bishop Yoder heaved out the words with a lot of gasping and gulping.

Noah laughed. "Bishop, did you run across the yard? We're not going to leave. I was giving Mary her wedding gift."

The bishop plunged his hand in his waistband, pulled out a handkerchief and patted his forehead. "I didn't want you escaping before the guests could actually see you two were married."

Mary shook a finger at the old man. "*Ach,* Bishop Yoder, it's a wonder we were ever married the way you were always trying to push me toward Seth."

The bishop laid his right hand on his heart. "Mary, you know I only want what's right for you. As you'll recall, I only relayed Seth's request to you. I never insisted you marry him. And what better way to get you to not marry Seth then to nudge you toward him? You are Sarah's *tochter* for sure and for certain. She, too, always went her own way. Sometimes *Gott* takes away so He can give you something that's right for you."

"*Mamm* was right, Bishop." Mary nodded. "You are an old softy."

The bishop jerked his chin in the air. "No one will ever believe that, and don't you repeat it. I have an image to uphold. So, Mary," Bishop Yoder changed the subject, "what will you do with Sweet Delights now?"

She glanced at Noah, and he raised a brow. "Noah is going to continue to help his *grossdaddi*, and I'm going to combine Sweet Delights with Noah's store, so to speak. We'll sell all the baked goods at Sweet Delights. Sarah plans to run the bakery with me, so we're combining the two families back into one bakery as it had been long ago. Did you see the sign that Noah hung in both our shops?

'Food nourishes the body on its journey, but it's love that gives the real taste to life.'"

The bishop nodded at Noah. "And will Jenny be joining the Amish as well?"

"*Nein*, Bishop, I don't think so. Jenny wasn't brought up in the Amish church and doesn't have the same urge to live among a family she doesn't know. She has picked a church that suits her. I was angry with God for taking our parents, and He was taking me on a journey to reconcile my heart back to Him." Noah squeezed Mary's hand. "And that led me straight to Mary."

"*Jah*, and what did you learn on this journey?"

"That God doesn't cause car accidents, men do. But God used the situation to bring my heart home to where it was meant to be."

Bishop Yoder patted Noah on the back. "*Jah*, but you had to find the right path. *Willkommen* to our community." He turned and headed back across the drive. "And don't be too long, you two. You have the rest of your lives together."

Noah pulled Mary back into his arms and pressed a long-overdue, tender kiss against her lips. "I love you, Mary."

"*Ich liebe dich*. I love you, Noah, with all my heart."

* * * * *

*If you loved this story,
check out more books from Marie E. Bast*
The Amish Baker
The Amish Marriage Bargain

Available now from Love Inspired!

*Find more great reads at
www.LoveInspired.com*

Dear Reader,

Thank you for traveling over the Washington County, Iowa, roads again to meet the Brenneman family. In *The Amish Baker*, Mary Brenneman was thirteen and her brother Jacob was six when baker Sarah Gingerich came into their lives. Now grown, Mary manages the Sweet Delights bakery for her stepmother.

However, Mary must work to save the bakery from competition with Noah Miller, an *Englischer* who's opened a grocery, delicatessen and bakery across the street. Although a strong-willed young woman, Mary meets her match when handsome, amber-eyed Noah Miller visits her bakery. While their professional lives clash, their constant contact brings them together in a relationship that could spell trouble, but God has a plan.

I love to hear from readers. Tell me what you enjoyed or what inspired you. Email me at Bast.Marie@yahoo.com, visit me at mariebast.blogspot.com; MarieBastAuthor. com; or facebook.com/marie.bast, or follow me on Twitter @MarieBast1.

Blessings,
Marie E. Bast